Chapter 1

"Now, can I check one mo.. ....
the toilet?"

Mary Plunkett closed her eyes and silently counted to ten. It was the third time Bernie had asked them and they hadn't even got on the train yet. Besides, didn't trains have toilets? It was three hours to their destination, and at the rate they were going Mary would have strangled her friend before they were halfway there.

"We're fine, Berns," Liz said. "Let's just get on the bloody thing before my water breaks."

"You're not that far along, are you?" A woman with blue eyeshadow and a high-pitched voice asked.

"No. I'm only six months."

"Ooh, you are carrying big, aren't you?" Blue eyeshadow said, and Mary was surprised that she had such a clear death wish.

"What exactly do you mean by –" Liz said, before Mary grabbed her arm.

"Look, here's our carriage," she said, firmly guiding her friend along the platform.

"I'm going to kill that woman," Liz muttered, "Did you know she tried to touch my hair earlier? Apparently she doesn't see much 'afro hair' in Pitlochry."

"Oh dear," Mary said. "I think she's just a bit out of her depth."

"In the ocean without a life raft, I'd have said," Bernie added. "Her name's Trystesse, if you can believe that. She was telling me earlier that she's Viola's cousin. And she's never met any of Viola's friends."

"Jesus, this hen-do is turning into a right joke," Liz said. "We barely know Viola, and it looks like no one else here does either. I don't know why we decided to come."

"Tax write off," Bernie said. "I told you, we got all that money from the police for the reports Liz did on the last case. I charged them a decent consultancy fee, and I need to spend some of the profits before the end of the tax year."

"Come on," Mary said, giving her friend's arm a squeeze. "A lovely hen weekend in a cottage with a hot tub and sauna. What could possibly go wrong?"

"Can't go in the hot tub. Or the sauna." Liz pouted.

Mary winced. "Listen, I've got cans of G&T in my bag... Oh."

Liz glowered at her.

"Maybe a nice soft drink."

Thankfully the train pulled up at that moment and the noise of it braking drowned out whatever choice words Liz was saying.

"I've bagged us a table," Bernie grinned when they made their way into the carriage. "An old lady with a cane was trying to

Death by Bedtime

The Wronged Women's Co-operative: Book 4

T E SCOTT

nab it but she couldn't hobble fast enough."

"Aren't we meant to be, you know, mingling with the rest of the hens?"

"Ha, I don't think so. That skinny girl from London just asked if I wanted any Prosecco. It's not even eleven a.m.!"

"Oh, I see," Mary said, checking that the cans of gin and tonic were hidden in her bag out of sight.

"I was hoping we could catch up on some paperwork for the WWC. Then we can turn it into an expense-deductible trip."

"Great," Mary said, her smile faltering a little. She sat down and straightened her dress over her knees. It was stripy with cats on it, and it was her new favourite thing.

"Now, who's got receipts for me?" Bernie asked.

While Liz scrolled through her online banking, Mary looked out of the window as the train pulled out of the central belt. Was it her imagination or was it already getting colder? She caught a glimpse of her reflection as they went through a tunnel. She was pleased with the way her magic wand earrings glinted in the light. One sand 'whizz' and the other 'bang'. Even Bernie had liked them. Well, she had said they were 'striking', which Mary was pretty sure was a compliment.

"Walker texted you yet?" Liz asked.

"I only saw him an hour ago," Mary replied.

"Aye, but you've only been going out a couple of months,"

7

Bernie said, pausing from tapping the keys of her laptop. "You're still in the 'can't live without each other for five minutes' stage."

"Well, he might have sent me a little love-heart emoji."

"Aw!" Liz said, while Bernie made finger down the throat movements.

"Come on Berns, even you and Finn must have been like that when you started going out," Liz said.

"We were not. I have never been the sentimental type."

"So how did you know you were going to marry him?" Mary asked, not able to resist.

"He fixed my overflow pipe," Bernie said. "It had been dripping for ages."

"That's what she said!" Mary said, at the same moment that Liz said the same thing. Then they collapsed into giggles.

"Idiots, both of you," Bernie said sternly, but they just ignored her.

"Good to see you're all having fun!" A perky London voice said. Mary looked up to see Hailey, the bridesmaid and chief hen-do organiser.

"The rest of us are in the next carriage, if you want to come along?" Hailey continued, either not noticing or just ignoring Bernie's icy glare.

"We've got a bit of work to do before the hen-do," Liz said.

"Oh yes, we've been hearing all about your little side-hustle. Any murders to solve today?"

"Not yet," Bernie muttered.

"We've just got some paperwork to go through," Mary said quickly as the first hint of a frown appeared on Hailey's brow.

"Well, we'll see you later then," the other woman said. She turned back the way she came, high heels clicking on the plastic floor.

"We really will have to join in soon," Mary said.

"What? You scared they won't like you?" Bernie asked.

"Not scared, exactly," Mary wriggled in her seat. The truth was, she was the sort of person that always wanted to be liked. As usual, Bernie spotted anyone's weakness and then held it up for the rest of the world to see.

"I wouldn't bother about them," Liz said. "Doesn't look like they've got a brain cell between them. When we got to the train station they were talking about what happened on EastEnders last night."

"Well, that doesn't make them stupid," Mary said.

Liz sighed. "You're right. I'm just grumpy. Hand me that bag, it's time to break out the snacks."

Mary watched as Liz pulled out an impressive collection of sweets and crisps from her handbag.

"And if you say anything about healthy eating in pregnancy,

9

Bernadette Paterson, I will shove this packet of crisps up your
—"

"I wouldn't dream of it," Bernie grinned. "Now let's get back to these expenses."

If there were groans around the table, Bernie pretended she hadn't heard them.

"This whole weekend is shaping up to be a nightmare," Liz scowled and put a hand on her rounded stomach. "I just hope I don't get motion sickness."

"We'll be there before you know it," Mary said, trying to sound cheerful.

"I've got to ask you, what's with all the witchy stuff?" Liz said.

Mary flicked her Gryffindor scarf back over her shoulder. "Well, it's the same train journey they take to Hogwarts. You know, over that big bridge thingy. So I thought I'd dress the part."

"Do you mean the Glenfinnan Viaduct?" Liz asked.

"Yes, that's the one."

"I hate to tell you this, but we're not going that way. That's on the West Highland Line."

"What?"

"Yeah, it goes over towards Fort William. We're heading for Aviemore."

"Bloody hell," Mary said, slumping back in her seat. "I was going to get you guys to act out the film with you two. I thought Bernie would make an excellent dementor."

"What was that?" Bernie asked, glancing up from her laptop.

"Never mind," Mary said, taking off her scarf and placing it into her bag. The earrings could stay though, she thought. They were cute.

"Let's start with last month's kitty," Bernie said. "Who bought the gin?"

Mary must have dozed off for a while, because the next thing she knew they were pulling into Aviemore station. She sat up and tried to surreptitiously wipe the drool from her chin.

"You were snoring like a trooper," Bernie said. The nurse had put away her laptop and was sitting with her arms folded.

"Sorry," Mary said. "Is it time to get off?"

"Yes," Liz said, putting snacks and a newspaper into her bag. "Let's make sure we remember our cases."

There was the usual awkward rush to get off the train, then they stood on the platform.

"Over here girls!" A voice trilled from their right.

Within meeting Bernie's eye, Mary trudged towards the other group. There were five of them including the bride-to-be. They had met the previous day during a cringe-worthy afternoon of cocktail making where everyone had been far too

11

sober to actually find it fun.

Viola was standing next to the bridesmaid, Hailey, who was shouting something about a taxi into her phone. Next to her was the unfortunately named Trystesse who was looking down at the ground. A few feet away were the two English women, Nora and Pru, and they were the ones that Mary found the most intimidating. They were younger, prettier and much posher than she was. They wore the sort of clothes that Mary only looked at in glossy magazines. Mary couldn't help it: she desperately wanted to be in their gang.

"Let's go join the raptors, shall we?" Bernie said, dragging her case behind her.

"Don't call them that, they might hear you," Mary whispered, but her friend didn't seem to notice.

"Taxi's waiting!" Hailey said, and they all trooped to the front of the station. The taxi was a minibus with a grumpy-looking driver smoking a cigarette.

The cool kids bagged the seats at the back of the minibus where they instantly started talking loudly about places in London none of the others had been to. Mary, Liz and Bernie squeezed into the seats behind the driver. Bernie wrinkled her nose and Mary just knew that she was going to go on an anti-smoking tirade, so she tried to think of something to say.

"Do you think we'll see some wildlife when we get there?"

"It's meant to be right out in the hills, isn't it?" Liz said. "Maybe we'll see a deer."

"I read the brochure," Bernie said. "They said that they had buzzards and squirrels nesting nearby."

"What's a buzzard? A type of squirrel?" Liz asked.

"Eagles, isn't it?" Bernie said. "I'm sure I read that somewhere."

"I'm hoping for some red squirrels. Maybe a wolf," Mary said.

"There's definitely no wolves," Liz replied.

"Are you sure?"

"Seventy per cent."

Bernie laughed. "We're a bit out of our depth here, aren't we? Too far north, if you ask me. You ever been up to the Highlands, Liz?"

"God no. Where did I put that sick bag?" she said, rummaging in her handbag. As one, Bernie and Mary shuffled further along the seats.

"Hang on a minute," Mary said. "You all live in Scotland, but none of you has been further up than Perth?"

"Don't be so smug," Bernie replied. "You only went to Aberdeen because your feckless ex dragged you there. How often did you go out into the Wilderness?"

Mary thought about it. "I went to Dundee once. That felt quite Wilderness-y."

Liz sighed. "So to sum up, we're all townies and we're all

probably going to get eaten by wildcats or drowned in a frozen loch somewhere. That's just great."

"You do know that wildcats are smaller than your average domestic tabby," Mary countered. "We're much more likely to get eaten by ravenous kilt-wearing Gaels."

The taxi driver coughed loudly.

"Probably best to wait until we're out of the car before you start insulting the locals," Liz hissed.

"I take your point," Mary whispered back.

Chapter 2: Liz

It took them an hour to get to the cottage. The last part of which was up single-track roads. It was only sheer willpower that had stopped Liz from needing to use the sick-bag she had clutched in her right hand.

"Nearly there ladies!" Hailey called from behind them. "If you've any phone calls to make, do it now. The reception is terrible, apparently."

Liz groaned. Why did the woman sound so cheerful about that? Too nauseous to make any calls, she sent a quick message sending love to Dave and Sean and promised to call them whenever she could. It did cheer Liz up a little that the Londoners were not happy about the lack of reception.

"What if work needs me?" Nora, the one wearing a beige jumpsuit, asked.

"I'm sure the nail salon can handle any emergencies without you," Viola said with an edge to her voice.

The rest of the journey passed in silence after that. By the time they got to the tiny lane that seemed to lead vertically up the mountain, even the taxi driver was swearing.

"Christ, you really are out in the sticks," he said, revving the engine to get them up the steep incline.

Liz clamped her teeth together, closed her eyes and tried to pretend she was somewhere else.

Finally, the sound of gravel under tyres told her they had arrived. The taxi pulled to a stop outside an old granite farmhouse.

"This is us, girls," Hailey said. "Isn't it quaint?"

"Does quaint mean drafty?" Bernie muttered as they climbed out of the car.

Mary arranged a whip-round to tip the driver, then the minibus drove away in a puff of gravel dust.

"Isn't it annoying how they call these things cottages," Bernie said as they dragged their suitcases up to the house. "I mean, it's a five bedroom detached house with a garage, not a bloody cottage."

"I suppose they think it sounds more picturesque," Liz said. She wasn't paying her friend much attention, all her focus now on getting inside and finding the loo. Being pregnant always made her feel like she was just a vehicle to push around a bladder.

"How do we get inside?" Viola asked.

"There's a lockbox with the keys. The owner lives half a mile away, he said he was going to try and be here, but if not to let ourselves in."

Hailey tapped the code into the metal box next to the door and a set of keys appeared.

"Bagsy first shot in the loo," Liz said as they shuffled inside. It wasn't until after she had used the facilities that Liz got a chance to appreciate where they were staying. An old farmhouse, it had been redecorated in the neutral-grey style that seemed to be the fashion at the moment. It was nice enough, if a little bland.

"Mary?" She shouted.

"Upstairs."

She found the others unpacking in the bedrooms. Liz and Mary were sharing a room with twin beds. It was cosy, in the way that meant very small, but the sheets were clean, so it would do just fine.

Without anyone discussing why, Bernie had been given a room to herself.

"I'm dying for a lie-down," Liz said. "Do you think –"

"Everyone in the kitchen in five minutes!" Hailey's voice called from downstairs.

"Never mind," Liz said, grabbing her comfortable slippers and putting them on her feet. They were already swollen from the journey.

"I hate to tell you this," Mary said. "But I think that Hailey is planning some games."

Liz's eyes flicked towards the ceiling for a second, but there was no escape there. She straightened her back. "We better go down."

Mary took her arm like they were walking in front of a firing squad. Or possibly going to the gallows.

They walked down the stairs to find the rest of the group in the kitchen. Hailey was pouring drinks, Viola, Nora and Pru were sitting around the dining table and Trystesse was staring out into the garden through the patio doors.

"Wine for everyone? Except you, of course, Liz. I've got some cola around here somewhere."

"I'll just grab a water," Liz said, forcing her face into a smile. "Or an orange juice if there is any."

"Actually, I was saving that for the breakfast bucks fizz tomorrow morning," Hailey said brightly. Liz looked into the woman's eyes, but couldn't see any sign that she was being deliberately antagonistic. The ever-present smile couldn't be natural, could it?

"Water is fine," Liz said, grabbing a glass.

"It's starting to snow," Trystesse said.

"Snow?" Liz walked over to the patio doors and sure enough, there was already a thin layer of white coating the garden. She couldn't believe her eyes. Maybe it was some sort of mirage, like when people saw Laurence Olivier in the desert or whatever. "It can't be snowing. It's April."

"Aye, that'll be the lambing snow," Trystesse said. "There's always a late snow to take the new lambs."

"What a cheery thought. I don't suppose you know when it'll

stop?"

The woman shrugged. "Looks pretty heavy right now. Don't think anyone will be going anywhere for a while."

Bernie staggered into the kitchen, groping for the kettle. "Have you looked outside?"

"Yes," Liz said, "and I'm not bloody happy about it."

Hailey grabbed her mobile. "Still no reception. There's a house phone somewhere." She hurried off out into the hall.

Liz checked her watch. It was going on for six o'clock. "Are we eating anytime soon?"

Viola got up from the table. "I think Hailey bought a load of frozen pizzas. She was going to do some party games first."

"Sod that," Liz said, opening the freezer, "some of us need to eat."

"I'm sorry if Hailey's a bit much," Viola said, her voice low. "I think it's the whole solicitor thing. She likes being organised."

"It's okay," Liz shrugged. "I mean, we all want you to have a good time."

"If I'm honest, I could have done without a hen-do altogether. After all, it's the wedding that's the important bit."

"How's the organisation going?"

Viola pouted. Liz wondered if she had had those lip-filler things people were always going on about. Her face was a little

19

too perfect, a bit too shiny. "The catering is a nightmare. Honestly, in London we would have no problem finding someone, but in Invergryff... Well, no one is coming up to scratch."

"Doesn't Alfie work in catering?" Liz asked, only half-remembering what it was that Viola's husband-to-be did. Viola worked in the school office, which is where they had all met.

"His parents own a hotel brand," Viola explained. "And yes, they have their own suppliers, but we wanted to go with someone local. I just don't think that's going to be possible, unless we want to serve Chicken Balmoral. And like I told the chef, it isn't 1986."

Liz laughed dutifully, although she was quite partial to a Chicken Balmoral, as long as she could add hot sauce to it.

Hailey came back into the room. "Well, I managed to get hold of the owner of the cottage. He says the snow should be gone by tomorrow. He's just half a mile up the track, so if we get stuck he'll come for us in his Land Rover."

"Is he handsome?" Nora asked, to a chorus of giggles.

"I couldn't tell over the phone, could I? Now, will we get started on the party games?"

Three hours later Liz had an inflatable tiara on her head, a phallic-shaped cookie in each hand and a terrible headache.

"I still say I'm winning," Viola said, waving her glass of fizz around so that it was raining onto the carpet. "That last question didn't count."

20

"Well, it's not my fault if Alfie thought that 'Relight my Fire' was your song," Hailey said. "He gave me the answers last week."

"As if I would like anything so cheesy. Our song is Frank Sinatra's 'Fly me to the Moon'. We're dancing it at the bloody wedding."

Liz glanced around the room. It was still early, but the party atmosphere was fading fast. Mary was fast asleep on the sofa and Bernie was doing the dishes.

"I thought you might like a tea," Trystesse said, handing a cup to Liz. "I made you a decaf one."

Touched, Liz managed a smile. "Thank you."

"Not really my thing, all these party games. I didn't even know you could do that with a hairdryer."

"I think we were all surprised by that one. And by the collection of blow-up items."

Someone had put 'Relight my Fire' on the music player and Viola was up dancing with Hailey, Pru and Nora.

"It's all Hailey's doing really," Trystesse said. "Apparently she's been a bridesmaid four times. Got it down to a fine art."

"Viola didn't ask you to be a bridesmaid?"

Trystesse giggled. Liz realised the woman was pretty drunk. "As if. I was surprised I even got an invite to the wedding. I think it's only because I still live in Scotland. Most of Viola's family are in France now. Somewhere near Nice. How do you lot know her?"

"She works at the school where our kids go," Liz explained. "I said to her one day that her nails were fab, and she offered to do mine. Sort of became friends from there." She didn't add that she, Bernie and Mary only really saw Viola once every couple of months. Liz felt sorry for the woman, about to get married with only a handful of real friends.

"Let's take a photo with the ring!" Pru said, and Viola held up her left hand while the others took selfies.

"Nearly two carats, can you believe it?" Viola said happily.

"You could poke someone's eye out with that," Pru laughed.

"It's not even the real one, is it?" Nora said, flopping down on the sofa.

"What do you mean?" Pru looked confused. Liz glanced over at Viola and saw that she had stopped dancing and was glaring at her friends.

"Oh come on, Viola must have told you the story. The first ring had a teeny tiny diamond, and she went off on one. Said it wasn't good enough, not for someone with Alfie's money. So she got her big diamond in the end."

Pru looked at Viola, then saw the anger on the other's woman's face. She took a step backwards.

"You weren't meant to tell anyone that," Viola hissed at Nora. The other woman just waved her hand and reached for her drink.

For a second, Liz thought it was all going to kick off. Hailey was staring at the rest of them, like she wasn't sure whose side to take. Then Viola cracked a smile.

"Ah, you're just jealous anyway. Look how it sparkles!"

She twirled around, pulling Pru into another dance just as Beyoncé came out of the speaker.

"I think I'll go to bed," Liz said.

Trystesse nodded. Her eyes were half-closed, but she didn't move from the seat.

"Bernie, would you help me get Mary up the stairs?"

When they woke Mary up, she just about managed to make her own way upstairs. Bernie took the opportunity to sneak off to her room and Liz collapsed into bed. Only two nights and then she would be back in her own bed, she thought. At least it couldn't get any worse. At which point Mary started to snore.

Chapter 3: Bernie

It was freezing when Bernie woke up at six o'clock. Even though she hadn't gone to bed until after eleven, she still got up and pulled on her dressing gown. She had always been an early riser, drilled into her through years of shift work. You got up, you got the work done early, and then you got a cup of tea. It was a simple life, but a fulfilling one. Or it had been, until she had started the WWC.

The Wronged Women's Co-operative had been started in anger. A friend of Bernie's who had been shafted by a husband who turned out to be not just a philanderer, but also a fraudster. One case had turned into another, then another. And Bernie had discovered that although she was a competent nurse, she was a brilliant investigator. She still worked the odd shift at the care home, but now the WWC was her full time job. And Liz's, not to mention providing part time employment for Mary Plunkett and Alice, Bernie's niece.

This hen-do was an annoying distraction from the work they were doing, but even Bernie saw the need for a change of scene. Besides, thanks to an incident with a duck pond, a cheating husband and six bags of instant noodles, they had cleared all their current cases.

Bernie had another reason for wanting some time away with her friends. Liz would be having a baby in a couple of months, and she had been putting some thought into asking Mary to take on more hours. She had started mainly as admin support, but it hadn't taken long for Mary Plunkett to become an integral part of the WWC. But was she up to stepping into Liz's patent high heels? Bernie wasn't sure.

"Breakfast!" a cheery voice called from somewhere downstairs.

Bernie smelled the bacon before she came into the kitchen where the ever-bubbly Hailey had laid out trays full of fried food. For a moment, Bernie had a wobble. It wasn't that long since she would have filled her plate with the stuff. But that wasn't what got her the title of Renfrewshire's best slimmer three months in a row.

"Just a coffee for me," she said, clicking the kettle on.

"Sore head today?" Hailey chirped.

"No. I only had a couple. Went to bed by eleven."

"That's right, you and the other Invergryff girls went to bed early."

"I think we're a bit old to be girls, don't you?" Bernie said.

"It's just a saying," Hailey replied, the perfect smile faltering.

"I mean, you're a lawyer, aren't you," Bernie continued. "Can't really imagine someone calling a lawyer a 'girl'."

"I'm a solicitor, not a lawyer."

"Right."

Pru and Nora walked into the kitchen, both pale-faced.

"Jesus, what was in those drinks last night?" Pru said, grabbing a roll and stuffing it with egg and bacon.

"We should have given up when we ran out of gin," Nora said. She turned away from the food and grabbed a jar of coffee. "Moving onto vodka was a stupid idea."

"What time did you go to bed?" Bernie asked.

"Three or four?" Pru said. "I don't even remember."

"I didn't think it was that late," Nora said, pouring the coffee and then slugging half of it back in one gulp. "You were in bed by then, weren't you Hailey?"

"Yes. Viola and I went up around two."

"She was in some state," Nora said.

"Well, it's her right as the bride-to-be, isn't it," Hailey said, but Bernie noticed that she didn't seem too impressed either.

Trystesse knocked on the door of the kitchen. "Okay to come in?"

Bernie rolled her eyes. The woman was the sort that would have asked permission to enter her own bathroom.

"There's food over here, Tryss," Hailey said.

"Thanks."

"Any sign of her? Viola I mean," Pru asked.

Trystesse shook her head. "I knocked on her door but there

was no answer. She had a fair bit to drink last night, I figured she needed the sleep."

"She was a total cow last night, you mean," Pru said. Bernie took another look at the Londoner. She looked worse than anyone else this morning, with grey skin and red wine-stained lips.

"She was just drunk," Nora said.

"That's no reason to bring up… to say what she did last night."

"And what was that?" Bernie asked.

"None of your business," Pru snapped back.

"Well, I'm afraid we're going to need Viola to get up," Hailey said. "We're meant to be axe throwing at midday. I do wish people had looked at the schedule. You did get the emails, didn't you?"

There was a chorus of not-very-enthusiastic assent.

"Right. I'm going to go and wake her up." Hailey stormed out of the kitchen, just as Mary and Liz walked in and started helping themselves to breakfast.

"Anyone got a ciggie?" Pru asked.

"I didn't know you smoked," Nora said.

"Gave up last year. But this being stuck in this bloody place feels like the perfect time to take it back up."

"Your lungs won't thank you for it," Bernie said.

Pru gave her a prize glare. Bernie was beginning to find these women rather annoying. Londoners, she had never particularly enjoyed them as a species, and these two were worse than most.

Bernie watched as Mary started to make herself a second bacon roll. The woman must have the metabolism of an ox to stay even remotely in shape, given her terrible diet. Was she... yes, to Bernie's horror she was going to add ketchup on top. Didn't she know it was just pure sugar?

Bernie watched the red ketchup drip onto the roll just as a piercing scream came from upstairs.

Mary dropped the bacon roll on the floor. In the kitchen, none of the women moved a muscle. Then there was a second scream.

It was Bernie who was first to move, jumping out of her seat and running for the stairs. That seemed to break everyone else out of their trance and the rest of them followed her.

The stairs were narrow and Bernie could hear the others banging into each other on the way up. She reached the top and looked around the landing. It didn't take long to find where the scream had come from.

Hailey was standing outside Viola's room, her hand out in front of her as if pushing away an attacker. Only there was no one there.

"What is it?" Bernie asked her.

Hailey just shook her head and pointed inside the room. Bernie stepped through the doorway, then paused.

"Stay back, everyone," Bernie said, and as she knew they would, they did exactly what she told them.

Death was nothing new for Bernie. Working in the care home she had seen more of it than most people. And she knew death wasn't always pretty. But there was something different about violent death, a life taken by force. Even though Violet was still in her bed, Bernie knew that that was what she was looking at.

Bernie walked into the room. She was hardly aware of the mess where someone had thrown open the suitcase and flung clothes all around the bedroom. She only had eyes for the figure on the bed.

Viola's eyes were open and her skin was cold, but Bernie took her pulse anyway. She had to be sure before she told the others, even though no one who has seen death mistakes it for anything else.

"She's dead," Bernie said, loud enough for the people outside to hear. There was a collection of wails and crying, but Bernie knew someone else could deal with that. She had a job to do here. She pulled up the sheets so that they covered Viola's face, but not before noticing two things. A half-drunk glass of water on the table next to the bed with just the hint of white powder in the bottom. And some drops of blood on a pillow next to the body.

"Bernie do you... is there anything I can do?" Liz called from the doorway.

Bernie stood up, feeling the creak in her knees as she did so.

"No. There's nothing we can do for her now."

"I'll call an ambulance," Mary said, pulling her phone out of her pocket. "Crap. No signal. Anyone got any?"

As each person checked their phone, an air of panic started to set in.

"No one's got any signal. And the internet is down too."

Without saying a word, Bernie walked past the bed and over to the window. She pulled the curtains open. Another couple of feet of snow had fallen. She couldn't even see the single-track road up to the cottage anymore.

"The snow must have knocked out the phone signal. And the broadband."

Hailey's voice was shrill. "Are you telling me that my friend is dead, and we can't even call for help?"

Bernie knew the women were seconds away from panic. She took a deep breath, then turned around to face the others.

"I think poor Viola had some sort of heart failure. She must have died in her sleep. It's very sad, but there's nothing we can do for her now. Let's go downstairs and make a plan."

As Bernie walked out of the room she saw her fellow WWC members looking at her. She gave them a discrete nod. Mary and Liz hadn't been fooled for a second. They knew fine well that there had been a murder. And that they were now sharing a house with a murderer.

Chapter 4: Walker

"That's two in the sandpit, one in the tree and three over by the gate trying to set a slide on fire."

"Are you sure that's all of them?" Sergeant Walker asked. "I don't want to lose a child."

"Nah mate," the seriously chilled-out Finn Paterson said. "Four of yours – well, Mary's, that is – one of mine and one of Dave's. We're sorted."

Walker slumped down into the plastic garden chair. "Thank god their dad is going to pick them up later. I don't know how you guys do this."

Finn handed him a beer. "Well, it's a bit easier when you've only got one."

Dave gave them a wave from over at the barbecue. "Five minutes for the sausages!" he shouted.

"Didn't he say that half an hour ago?" Walker asked, swallowing some of the cold beer.

"Just as long as they're not the usual black on the outside, raw in the middle. I once gave Bernie a bad dose of salmonella after I tried to do jerk chicken wings on the barbeque. I'd been watching that Jamie Oliver do them. She didn't speak to me for a week."

Laughing, Walker took another drink. He didn't mention that

if he was married to Bernie Paterson, he would have been glad of the silence.

A chill wind from the north made him pull his coat around his chest more tightly. Dave had been determined that there needed to be a barbeque while the wives were away, and the fact that it was barely ten degrees wasn't going to stop him.

"How do you think they're getting on up North?" Finn asked.

"I spoke to Mary yesterday and they seemed to be having a good time. It's a bit awkward though as no one seems to really know each other."

"If it was blokes we'd all be best pals within five minutes."

Walker chuckled. "Or punching each other's lights out. No, I think the issue is that there are the mums that know Viola from school, then there are her university pals, and neither group is speaking to each other. Liz is fed up because she can't drink and Bernie is…" he trailed off.

Finn laughed. "Aye, she's an acquired taste. I know my wife, and it definitely takes people a while to warm up to her. Aviemore won't know what's hit it."

Dave wandered over from the barbecue with a couple of plates. "Here's some burgers. You might want to eat them before the kids munch them all."

Walker glanced up to see Mary's son Peter drop his sausage on the ground, then pick it up and eat it. He pretended not to notice.

"Thanks." The burger was surprisingly good, and not raw in the middle.

"How's it going with the kids?" Dave asked.

"Not too bad. I mean, they tolerate me. Seem more interested in whatever's on the telly than their mum's new boyfriend, and to be honest that suits me fine."

"What do they call you, Uncle?"

"They just call me Walker."

Dave laughed. "Does anyone use your first name?"

Walker flinched. "Well, not really. It started at Police College. They were calling me shortbread, for obvious reasons, and then that petered out, and they settled for Walker."

"Aye, it is funny how these things work out," Dave said. "I've got a pal who has been called Frodo since he was ten, and none of us can remember why. Nearly died at his wedding when we found out his first name was Archibald."

Finn nodded. "It's a lot more polite than the nicknames you hear onsite, that's for sure."

"Can we have an ice-cream?" Vikki appeared from nowhere, a ketchup grin making her look like a tiny female Joker.

"Sure," Dave said. "There's a load in the freezer. Get Sean to help you find them."

"And eat an apple after," Walker added. "Your mum said you had to get your five a day."

34

Vikki gave him a perfect eye roll, then turned and ran into the kitchen.

"How's work going?" Finn asked. "Bernie told me to tell you to save any murders for when she got back."

Walker laughed. "Funnily enough, as soon as the WWC headed out of Invergryff we've not had a single murder. I'm sure that says something."

"You'll be enjoying the time off then?"

"Not really. There's been a load of burglaries in Kennilworth. At the one last week they beat up one of the homeowners pretty badly. We're hoping we get them before they kill someone."

That chilled the atmosphere for a few minutes.

"I better check on the kids," Dave said. "Make sure they've not decimated the freezer."

Walker checked his phone. No messages or calls from Mary. "Have you heard from Bernie today?"

Finn shook his head. "No, but Dave was saying that Liz had told him the reception up there was meant to be crap. So that he wouldn't worry about her and the baby."

"She's still got a few months to go though, doesn't she?"

"Aye."

Dave came back outside. "They're ransacking the living room now. I think they're turning it into a fort, and we're outnumbered."

"You heard from Liz today?" Walker asked him.

"Nah, no reception."

"And you're not worried about... you know, the baby when you can't get in touch with her."

Dave grinned. "I never worry about Liz. I've never met anyone who is anywhere near a match for her. Even Bernie."

"True," Finn said.

"What do you think they're getting up to right now?" Walker asked him.

"Probably having a whale of a time without kids and husbands to annoy them."

Walker checked his phone again. He thought that Mary might have text him by now, at least a silly gif or some comment about all the TV shows she was missing. But maybe he was just being too needy. She was probably having the time of her life.

Chapter 5: Mary

Mary was trying to be very cool about the fact that there was a dead body in the house. She was doing her absolute best to be a cold, rational investigator, the sort of person that Bernie Paterson would be proud of. If only she could stop her eyes from leaking.

You didn't even like her, she told herself, but somehow that made it worse. Poor Viola. Had any of them really liked her? It had been her hen-do and no one seemed to want to be there. And now someone had disliked her enough to kill her.

"Jesus, I wish I'd brought more of those anti-sickness pills," Liz said, emerging from the bathroom.

"Are you all right?"

"Yeah. You ever seen a dead body before?"

Mary shook her head.

"Me neither. I didn't think it would be so... real. You know?"

Mary did, and her stomach lurched again to tell her that it knew too.

There was a knock at the door. Hailey popped her head in. She had lost her characteristic smile and mascara coated her cheeks.

"Bernie needs a hand in the... you know, in Viola's room."

Mary and Liz trudged after her towards the bedroom. Bernie was standing in the doorway.

"We need to do something about Viola," Bernie said.

"What do you mean?" Mary asked, although she had a feeling she knew.

"We need to get her out of here," Bernie replied.

"We shouldn't move her at all," Liz said sternly. "The police won't be happy if we mess up the crime scene."

"I think we've probably done that already," Bernie pointed out. "And I'm worried about the effect of the central heating. If it's going to be a couple of days before anyone gets out here…"

"It won't be, will it?" Mary asked, horrified. She hadn't even considered that they might be stuck here for that long.

"We have to consider the worst case scenario," Bernie said."

"Yeah, and there's no way I can stay in this house while it's got a… while she's just lying there," Hailey added.

"Do you think… could we put her outside?" Mary asked. "The snow would keep her cold."

Bernie shook her head. "No. There are the wild animals to consider."

Hailey put her hand to her mouth and then ran back along the corridor.

"Then what should we do?" Liz asked.

"There's a garage attached to the house. I saw it when we came in. As long as we can lock it, I think we should put her in there. We can take off the bedsheet and move her in that."

"And you want us to help?"

"She's not very heavy. Between the three of us, we can lift her. If you're up to it, Liz?"

"I'll manage," Liz said. Mary was impressed. Liz had the perfect excuse of pregnancy to avoid this horrible job, but she was going to do her bit. And if she could do it, Mary would too. Even if the thought made her shudder.

Half an hour later, the body of Viola Gordon had been laid in the garage, behind a stack of empty cardboard boxes. It didn't seem very respectful, but then what was the alternative? At least it was cold enough to keep her preserved for when the police finally turned up.

The thought of the police made Mary check her phone. Still no signal or internet. In a way that was becoming something of a tic, she went to the window and looked outside. Still white, snow still falling, still impossible to leave.

They trudged back into the house where the others were gathered in the kitchen. Trystesse was curled up in the corner, staring out at the snow. Nora, Pru and Hailey were sitting around the table.

"Did you get it... her, moved okay?" Hailey asked.

"Yes," Bernie said. "Now, I think we need to decide what to do next."

Trystesse turned around, her eyes red-rimmed. "Shouldn't we just wait for the phone signal to come back?"

"How long will that be?" Bernie asked. "Could be hours or days from what I can tell. I suggest that Mary and I try and walk to the nearest house to get help. Liz will stay here and take your statements."

"Our statements?" Trystesse bit her lip.

"Yes. The police will want them, and it's better to get them down while the memories are fresh."

"What can we tell the police?" Hailey asked. "She died while we were all asleep. It's a tragic accident."

Bernie didn't reply.

"You don't think it was an accident? But you said it was."

"We can't know anything for sure yet. Look, Hailey said that the owner of the cottage is just further up the road, is that right?"

Hailey nodded. "Half a mile, he said."

"Okay, so Mary and I will try to get there through the snow. Hopefully, he'll have a phone that works, if not we'll come back with him in his Land Rover and we can all drive to the nearest police station together, right?"

At the mention of the Land Rover the women cheered up a

little.

"Sooner we get out of here the better," Pru said. "Will you two be okay in the snow?"

"We'll take our time," Bernie said, which Mary realised was not the same as saying 'yes'. "Can we borrow any coats that look warm? Mary doesn't have one."

"I didn't know I was going to be hiking in the snow," Mary grumbled.

"Take mine. It's a Barbour one," Nora said.

"Help yourselves to anything," Hailey said. "I mean, it's all to help Viola, right?"

"Think she's beyond help now," Pru said, earning her a glare from the others.

"All right. Liz, can you help us get ready?"

Liz followed them out into the hall.

"I'm going to need you to keep an eye on them," Bernie whispered to their friend. "Let me know if they say anything relevant."

"I will do," Liz said, although she didn't look very happy about it. "Look, I better get back in there in case they're talking about you."

Liz went back into the kitchen and pulled the door behind her.

Mary pulled on the green Barbour jacket. It went down to her knees, but at least it was warm. "Are you sure we should be doing this?"

Bernie pulled on a coat and gloves. Her face was hard, business-like. "Yes."

"The thing is, Bernie, if we leave now, we're leaving Liz with a murderer."

Bernie nodded. "I know. And I've weighed up the risks. But it seems to be it's more of a risk for a pregnant woman to trudge through the snow for hours than to be in a house with a killer."

"Shouldn't we let Liz make that decision?"

"No point worrying her," Bernie said. "Let her get on with her job. She can take care of herself."

Chapter 6: Liz

In the kitchen of the cottage, Liz was doing her best to not be upset that her friends had abandoned her to a murderer.

"Pru, why don't you come with me and we can write down your statement."

Hailey sniffed. "I don't see why we need to do this with you."

"I have given statements to the police several times," Liz said, keeping her voice calm. "It makes sense if I do it."

"Just because you think you're Nancy Drew, doesn't mean you get to boss us around," Nora said.

"True. And you're free to find someone else to help you. Of course, that might be a bit tricky given that we're trapped here for the foreseeable future."

Pru stood up. "I'll come and do the statement, for what it's worth. Might as well get it out of the way."

"Good. Let's go to the living room. If the rest of you could stay in the kitchen, just in case that phone starts working."

They all stared at the phone on the table as if willing it to ring. It didn't.

"Fine," Hailey said, "but I'm opening a bottle of wine."

Liz shrugged. She could hardly stop them from drinking, and

saying something like 'best to stay sober if there's a murderer about' might have caused a little panic.

She got up and walked to the living room, Pru following behind her. Liz made sure to shut the door behind them so that the others couldn't listen in. Was it paranoia when you were living with a potential murderer? Or just a legitimate precaution.

Liz rummaged in her bag until she found a notebook.

"Do you think the others will be okay?" Pru said. She was sitting on the edge of the sofa, her legs crossed and her arms folded. She had the sort of figure that Liz had envied in her teens, before she had realised that that level of skinny was never going to happen with her African genes.

"As long as they stay in the kitchen," Liz said.

"You're making sure that none of us are alone, aren't you?"

Liz swallowed. "Yes."

"So you don't think she died in her sleep? You think that one of us killed her?"

"I hope not," Liz said, deciding that honesty was the best policy. "But while it's a possibility, don't you think it's a good idea to be careful?"

"I think it's every woman for herself," Pru replied. "How do I know that it wasn't one of your little detective club that killed her? You hardly knew Viola at all."

"You've known her for years, haven't you?"

Pru nodded. Her hair was pulled into a tight bun but she smoothed it back anyway. "We all went to college together. Business studies. One of those courses that you do when you can't decide what to do with your life. We were in the same class and just hit it off."

"This was in London, right? Why did Viola go down there if she was Scottish?"

"Her mum's from up here, but her dad's a Cockney. She spent half the year in each place. It wasn't until she met Alfie that she moved up to Invergryff permanently."

Liz nodded. It was irritating to her how little she knew about the dead woman. After all, they were supposed to be friends. Liz realised she would have to get to know her quickly, if she wanted to find out who killed her.

"And you're from London?"

"Just outside. Deepest darkest Surrey. As soon as I could I left suburbia for the big city. College was just the start, after that I started my HR firm, and now I manage a team of fifty people."

"Wow," Liz said, genuinely impressed. "But you still kept in touch with Viola and Nora?"

Pru picked at the end of her nail. "Sort of. I mean, we'd meet up once or twice a year. It was Nora that kept it going, really. Sometimes I would send clients her way. She owns a beauty room in London, hair and nails and Botox, that sort of thing.

Viola would meet up with us when she was down in London visiting her dad. To be honest, I was surprised to get an invite to the hen-do."

"You're not the first person to say that. Why do you think Viola didn't have more close friends?"

"Well, that thing about living between Scotland and England can't have helped. And she could be difficult sometimes. I guess you might call her a bit of a bitch. I know that sounds bad now, but I'm just being honest. Especially since she got together with Alfie."

"What changed then?"

The other woman sighed. "Okay, so she was always the one that struggled for money. I mean, she worked in a school, so it wasn't exactly well paid. Then she got her rich boyfriend and everything changed. She was posting online all the time about her fancy holidays and her new clothes. The last time she came down to London she insisted on going to this swanky restaurant, cost two hundred quid per person. I mean, I've done all right for myself, but I don't like to rub it in other people's faces. Nora was kind of annoyed about it."

"Annoyed?"

"As in, she sent me some snarky messages afterwards. Not as in she would want to kill anyone."

"I didn't mean that."

"I know exactly what you meant. Can we get on with the statement?"

"Alright. Tell me what happened from the time we got to the cottage."

"You know all this."

"I know, but the police don't."

With much complaining, Pru detailed their movements when they arrived at the cottage up until eleven at night.

"Now this is where I'm not sure what happened," Liz said, "the rest of us went to bed at eleven, but you, Trystesse, Nora, Hailey and Viola stayed up, is that right?"

"Yeah. We were all bitching about how flaky you lot were, by the way."

"Flaky? I'm pregnant."

"Just an excuse, that's what Viola said. Hey, maybe you killed her."

"That's not very funny."

"I'm not joking," Pru said. She leaned forward and Liz could see the fine lines around her eyes that makeup had hidden yesterday. "I don't know you. Just because you and your friends run a detective agency, doesn't mean we should all follow you blindly to… well, wherever. As far as I'm concerned, you're just as likely to have hurt Viola as the rest of us are. More, in fact."

"What do you mean 'more'?"

"Well, who is more likely to know how to get away with

murder than someone who deals in it all the time?"

There was a weird sort of logic to this that Liz could hardly deny.

"You're going to have to trust someone, Pru," she said after a moment's thought. "And me, Mary and Bernie might be your best bet. Because I know that none of us would kill Viola."

"Know, as in a hundred per cent? You can't be sure, can you? I mean, one look at that Bernie woman would tell you that she would do absolutely anything to get her own way."

"Bernie doesn't have a motive," Liz said, almost laughing at the absurdity of it.

"Neither do I."

Liz took a deep breath. "Tell me what happened in the kitchen after eleven."

"Hailey insisted on playing more drinking games. Shots of gin. She made us play 'I Never'."

"That's the one where you say something that you've never done and if the others have then they have to drink?"

"Exactly. It was a good laugh at first, but then Viola started picking on that Tryss girl."

"Picking on her how?"

"Well, it was kind of obvious that Tryss hadn't done much. Viola started doing stuff like I've never had sex outside, you know, that sort of thing. And Tryss hadn't done any of it.

48

Which was fine, I mean, who cares, but Viola kept pushing her to admit she had done something. Eventually, Tryss got annoyed and wandered off."

"There wasn't a row?"

"No, nothing that bad. Just stupid drunken stuff"

"Was Viola having a go at anyone else?"

"No."

"What happened then?"

"Then we put music on and everyone was just sort of chatting. Hailey and Tryss were on the sofa, and the rest of us were sat at the table. Still drinking which is why my head is bloody awful today."

"When did each of you go upstairs?"

"Tryss was next I think, although I couldn't tell you what time, I only noticed because Hailey came over to join us. Then Viola and Hailey went upstairs just before two. I know that because I looked at my phone to check the time, and saw that there was still no bloody reception." Pru took her phone out on reflex, checked it, and then shoved it back into her pocket.

"And you and Nora stayed up?"

"Yes, for about an hour."

"What were you talking about?"

"None of your business."

49

"Fair enough. Now here's the important bit. When you went upstairs, did you realise anything was wrong?"

Pru rubbed her knuckles into her eye sockets. "I didn't see anything. I think… I was totally plastered, remember? But I think all the doors to the bedrooms were shut. Nora showed me which one was ours and we went in and basically collapsed into bed. I didn't even take my makeup off."

"Did you go out again to go to the bathroom?"

"No. We have an en-suite in the room."

"And you didn't hear or see anything unusual?"

"Like what?" Pru pulled at a loose piece of hair, tucking it back behind her ear. "Someone being murdered? No, I had no bloody idea anything had happened until we all went into her room this morning."

Liz put her pen down. "I guess that's it then. If you think of anything else –"

"Then I'll tell an actual police officer," Pru said. "Your friends better make it through the snow."

"I'm sure they will," Liz said with more confidence than she felt.

"They better. Otherwise we've lost another two people and that's only improving the odds for the murderer."

"You're sure it's one of us, then," Liz said.

Pru laughed. "I'm not an idiot. Who else could it be?"

Liz felt a kick in her belly and all of a sudden her mouth went dry. "I don't know. But I'm going to find them whoever they are. You can be sure of that."

Chapter 7: Bernie

Walking through a blizzard was exactly as tricky as you might think. Although the snowfall wasn't that heavy, the way it swirled around was disorientating. But when they first stepped out of the house, Bernie thought it was almost peaceful. The sound-deadening quality of snow meant the only thing she could hear was her footsteps and the constant grumbling of Mary walking behind her.

"My cheeks are freezing," the woman said, stomping through the snow like an angry toddler.

Bernie ignored her. She had to concentrate on not losing her footing. Under the thick snow, there was a layer of black ice on the road, and she had already fallen on her arse twice.

A bird tweeted somewhere, in a way that sounded like it was mocking them.

"It's a pity about all the trees," Bernie said after a few minutes of quiet. "Probably be a nice view if you could actually see anything."

"Trees are kind of a thing in the countryside," Mary said. "Although it does make it a bit creepy. Do you think… could someone have hidden here, then come into the house to kill Viola?"

"No," Bernie said. "I checked this morning. There was no water on any of the floors."

"Sorry, what does that mean?"

"It had already started snowing yesterday. By the time Viola was killed there was at least a foot of snow all around the cottage. No way could anyone have come in without leaving watery footprints everywhere."

"They could have taken off their shoes."

"There would still have been a few drops from their clothes. I checked everywhere. It was bone dry."

Mary slipped for a second, then righted herself. "Then it was one of us that killed her."

"Not one of us," Bernie said firmly, "one of them."

They walked on in silence for a while. Bernie was not normally someone troubled by conscience, but she was feeling increasingly bad about leaving Liz behind.

"You're sure it couldn't have been an accident? Or… suicide?"

"You've asked me that three times already."

"Tell me again," Mary said, her breath puffing out in a cloud. "It is kind of important."

"The glass next to her bed had some sort of powder at the bottom of it. Someone had definitely put something in her drink."

"Could you tell what it was?"

"No. I sniffed it but it didn't smell of anything. But I think she was smothered too."

"Because of the blood on the pillow?"

"Yes. I think it was pushed into her face with enough force that she was asphyxiated. The lack of oxygen and the force could cause blood vessels to burst and…"

"I see," Mary said quickly. "Let's move on, then. If we're sure that she was killed, and we know it wasn't by someone outside of the house, then it must be one of four people."

"Nora, Pru, Trystesse and Hailey."

"The women that we've just left Liz with."

"Yes. But the way I see it, the killer was only interested in Viola."

"How do you work that one out?"

"Well, we were all asleep in our beds last night, half of us so drunk we wouldn't wake up if a herd of elephants came into the room. So if they had wanted to murder everyone, they would have done it last night."

"What a lovely thought," Mary said. "Ugh, I've just stepped into the ditch. Now my socks are soaking."

"Serves you right for having such silly boots."

"Well, I thought I was going to be sipping champagne in a hot tub, not trekking through a forest to try and find a phone. Which way from here?"

They had reached a fork in the road.

"I remember on the satnav it goes west from here," Bernie said, taking the right-hand fork.

"And which way is west? Or do you have a bloody compass on you?"

Really wishing she had brought Liz along instead, Bernie turned to face Mary. She could only see the woman's eyes peeking out from the red and yellow scarf she had wrapped around her face.

"If you look at the sun at midday that's south." Bernie pointed. "It's just after twelve so that's good enough. West is this way."

"Bloody hell Bernie, is there anything you can't do."

"Crochet. Never got the hang of the little hooks."

They trudged along the track, the fence on their right guiding them along.

"I wish Walker was here. Or any police officer for that matter. I can't help feeling that we were wrong to move the body."

Bernie shrugged. "We did what we had to do. If I'd left her in the bed the others would have panicked. That's the last thing we need right now."

"I guess. Man, it is cold out here. Are you sure we're going the right way?"

Bernie just kept walking. She didn't understand Mary's need to constantly question everything. Either they were going the right way or they weren't. What was the point in worrying about it?

"Do you think the snow is getting heavier? I can't feel my toes. If only there was a car or a dog walker or something."

At the end of her tether, Bernie turned to snap at Mary, then spotted something. "You might be in luck," she said, peering through the trees. "I think I've found a house."

Five minutes later they were ringing the bell of a single-storey house with Land Rover parked in the drive.

For a moment Bernie thought no one was going to answer, but then the door opened.

"I was just coming down to see you," a man in his sixties with grey stubble and a weathered face said. "I thought you might be in trouble."

"You know about the murder," Mary gasped, before Bernie could say anything.

"Murder?" The man frowned. "I meant the snow. What's all this about a murder."

Bernie sighed. "Do you have a working phone?"

"Afraid not. It's all gone down. Might take them days to get the line back up. Been a long time since the snow's been this bad at this time of year."

"We don't have time for that," Bernie said. "Can you take us somewhere with a phone? We need to speak to the police."

"You weren't joking about a murder then?" he asked, staring at them.

"No."

"Bloody hell. You better come in and get warmed up."

"We need to get to town."

"Aye, but there's no point if you freeze to death first. Besides, I'm going to have to dig the car out. That's not going to be a five minute job. Come inside and get a hot drink in you."

Bernie looked at Mary and shrugged. They didn't seem to have much of a choice.

"I'm William Laurel," the man said as he led them into the hall and helped them take off their coats. "This is my farm."

"You're the one that rented the cottage out, is that right?" Bernie pulled off her boots, leaving wet puddles on the tiles.

"Aye. Your friend Hailey booked it."

"How did she find it?"

"Oh, we're on all the usual websites. We advertise for people looking for something more out of the way than your usual trip. Want to get away from civilisation for a weekend, that sort of thing."

"Handy for a murderer, when you think about it," Bernie said.

"That's not exactly our fault," William said, straightening up. "You're sure that someone was killed, then? It wasn't an

57

accident?"

Mary was rubbing her hands together to warm them up. "It was Viola, the bride-to-be. Someone killed her in her bed. We think she was –"

"We need to wait for the police to take a look," Bernie said, before Mary could say any more. "But it looks like she was deliberately killed."

"I just can't believe it. My wife is going to be very upset."

"So are Viola's family," Bernie said, with an edge to her voice.

"Yes, of course," William ran a hand across his forehead. "It's just… well, normally my wife does the holiday lets, but she's away in Spain at her mother's house so I said I would take care of this one. It's not going to look very good for the business, is it?"

"You were going to dig out the Land Rover," Bernie prompted, finding the self-pity irritating.

"Of course. I'll just make you a tea –"

"We can do it ourselves, if you sort the car."

"Of course. I'll get on and do that then, shall I?"

"Yes." Bernie watched while he pulled on his coat and headed out the door. Mary clicked the kettle on and started the search for mugs. Everything was in hand, but when Bernie looked out of the window she felt an uncharacteristic pang of self-doubt. Bernie Paterson wasn't scared of anything, but for the first time she knew she was out of her depth. The Scottish weather was one thing that she couldn't bully into submission. But she was going to have a jolly good try.

Chapter 8: Walker

The barbecue was still going strong when it was time for Walker to take the kids to their grandmother's. He bundled them all into the car and only had to make three trips back to the house for lost coats, forgotten toys and in one memorable case, to return a barbecue skewer that was being used in an attempt to impale a sibling.

The short drive to Mary's mother's house was pleasant enough as the sound of eighties Rock from the car speaker was louder than the bickering from the back seat. By the time they pulled up outside the tidy little house in a quiet cul-de-sac, they were all doing the head bang from Bohemian Rhapsody. For a moment Walker felt quite smug about his parenting-adjacent afternoon. Then Peter pulled Vikki's hair and the screaming started again.

"Time to go to granny's house," he said, encouraging them all out of the car and up the drive to the house. A woman that was an older version of Mary, only with a more conservative dress sense, opened the front door.

"Where are my little angels?" Nel said as the children ran into the house, babbling away at a hundred miles an hour.

"I think I probably let them have too much sugar," Walker said as he walked up to her.

"Ah, they're at their grannies now, they can have what they like. Do you have time for a cuppa?"

Walker looked down at his feet. He had only met the woman once before and it was still a little awkward. He wasn't entirely sure how she felt about her daughter's new boyfriend.

"Sorry, I've got to get off. I'll get the car seats for you."

"Have you heard how Mary's getting on?"

Walker shook his head. "The reception is bad up there. Dave and Finn haven't heard anything either."

A frown creased Nel's forehead. "I just saw on the forecast that the weather is bad up there. A snowstorm, by the sounds of it."

"Really?" It seems amazing to Walker that the weather could be that bad just a hundred miles away.

"Do you think… they will be all right, won't they?"

"I'm sure they will," Walker said.

Nel attempted a smile. "You never stop worrying about them. Children I mean. Even when they're all grown up. I guess that's something that… well, you won't know that yet."

He shrugged off the comment. "I'll keep trying Mary. If I get through to her I'll let you know."

"Thanks," Nel said, already distracted by some fractious voices in the house behind her.

Walker took the car seats out of his car, noting with displeasure the sticky residue left on the leather. Why were kids always sticky? It was a mystery worthy of top scientists,

61

but no one had ever found a reason.

He left the car seats next to the front door and gave the kids a wave through the living room window. Back in his car, he checked his phone. No messages from Mary. He did have a missed call from Dave, Liz's husband.

For a minute, Walker wondered if he had left something behind at the barbecue. Maybe one of the children. But then he remembered that he had been careful to count them.

He called Dave.

"Sorry to bother you," the other man said. "I was just wondering if you had heard anything from Mary?"

"Not so far," Walker replied. "I've sent her a couple of texts but no reply."

"Right." There was a pause on the other end of the phone. "It's just… I feel stupid even for saying this, but Liz normally phones to check in whenever she's away, but no calls so far. I'm probably just paranoid because of the baby."

"Don't worry about it. I'm sure they'll call soon."

"Yeah. You managed to offload the kids okay?"

Walker grinned. "Haven't lost one yet."

"Good job mate."

Dave clicked off the call and Walker sat in the car for a moment, a frown appearing between his eyebrows. He opened the glove compartment and took out his work phone, then he called the office.

"Isn't it your day off?" Sergeant Neil Mickelson said when he picked up the phone.

"Yes. Can you do me a favour?"

"Depends what it is," Neil chuckled.

"Can you check if there are any reports of any accidents, any police incidents up Aviemore way?"

Walker heard the clacking of keys in the background. "Nothing out of the ordinary. A couple of trees down with the snow, but the fire service is dealing with that. Something the matter?"

"No," Walker said, already feeling foolish for asking. "Just checking on something."

"It wouldn't be the girlfriend, would it? Take it from me, they don't like it when you check up on them."

"It's not like that, the weather is bad and there's no reception, that's all."

"I'll let you know if anything comes in," Neil said, and Walker was grateful that he didn't take the Mickey out of him for being anxious.

"Thanks. I owe you a beer." Walker clicked off the call and pulled out of Nel's drive. He put the Queen album back on the radio, but it wasn't the same without the backing vocals. He had managed a day alone with the kids, and he couldn't even call Mary to let her know he had survived. That was the only reason for the nervous shiver he felt creeping up the back of his neck. He was sure of it.

Chapter 9: Mary

Riding in the Land Rover was exciting. If Mary squinted, she could pretend she was in a Bond movie. The sixty-year-old driver who smelled of stale cigarettes wasn't quite the action hero she might have imagined. Still, each time they reached a bend and the tyres crunched into fresh snow, she had to resist the urge to go 'Weee!'"

Both her and Bernie were sitting in the back seat, their phones in their hands. William had told them that sometimes there were patches of reception, but it didn't seem to be working today. As he explained it, his farm and the cottage got their internet access from a private signal, and the snow had taken it out. Phone reception didn't often fail at the same time, but it looked like the weather had killed that too. Mary wondered if it was all a little convenient. Maybe William himself had cut them off somehow, to enable him to kill Viola. But then, what was his motive? He had never even met the woman.

"Damn, it's bad here. There's ice under this snow," William said, and suddenly the car ride didn't seem quite so fun. Mary could see him fighting with the wheel.

Mary looked at Bernie, but the nurse was glaring out at the snow, as if the Scottish weather was a naughty patient that hadn't been taking its meds. Still, even though she could be a bossy cow, Mary was glad that Bernie had been there when they found the body. No one else would have managed to deal with it in such a calm and considered way. It was only the fear of letting Bernie down that was keeping Mary from losing it altogether. After all, she had never seen a dead body before, and certainly not of someone she knew.

Poor Viola. They didn't seem to be any closer to knowing who killed her. Despite what Bernie had said, Mary couldn't resist thinking that some intruder could have come in and killed her. It made so much more sense than the idea that one of the women she had been sharing crisps and dip with last night was a murderer. Or a murderess. Or was that sexist these days?

"What are you thinking?" Bernie asked.

"Murderer or murderess?"

"What?"

The wipers were moving so quickly it was mesmerizing.

"Do you think Liz is okay?"

"I'm sure she's fine," Bernie said, but she looked out of the window again.

Mary chewed her thumbnail. "Shouldn't we be at the cottage by now?"

"I'm having to crawl along these roads," William said, "if we're lucky we'll make it to the cottage without hitting a tree, but there's no way we're going to Aviemore."

"What?" Bernie's head whipped around to face the driver.

"It's too dangerous. Look, the snow is still coming down, and it's heavier than it was this morning."

"Does the whole 'there's been a murder in your cottage' thing not bother you?" Bernie snapped.

"Of course it does," William said, pulling the car out of another skid. "Look, here's the cottage. Let's see if we can… damn!"

The Land Rover lurched to the right and Mary grabbed onto her seat. They tipped over at a forty-five degree angle.

William swore loudly, then opened the door and jumped out. Bernie did the same, and Mary took a deep breath and then climbed out after them.

"Stuck," the man said, stating the obvious. The Land Rover had gone off the edge of the road and two of its wheels were floating in the air. The snow was already starting to cover the skid marks.

"Let's get up to the house," Mary said, walking quickly as the snow settled in her hair. She had a horrible feeling that they had been wrong to leave Liz behind. She was imagining the worst sort of horror movie where they would return to the house only to find a knife-wielding killer and bloodstains on the walls.

Despite Bernie having the longer stride, Mary's panic meant that she was first to the cottage. She tried the front door but it was locked. Adrenaline racing through her veins, she rang the doorbell and slammed her palm against the door.

It was several long seconds before it opened.

"Bloody hell, Mary, I was making a cuppa," Liz said, and her face turned to one of surprise when Mary wrapped her into a hug.

"Thank goodness you're okay."

"She won't be if you keep squeezing the air out of her," Bernie grumbled as she pushed past, pulling off her boots.

"Is this the cavalry?" Liz asked, introducing herself to William Laurel.

"Cavalry without the bloody horse," William grumbled. "Jesus, what temperature have you got this place at? The thermostat was set at eighteen."

"I think we're paying enough to warrant turning the heating on," Hailey said, appearing from the kitchen.

William frowned, but didn't argue. "Where's the... the lass that died."

"We put her in the garage," Bernie said. "It's nice and cold in there."

"I hope you're going to be taking us all to the police station," Hailey said. "We're all packed and ready to go."

"I'm afraid you're going to have to unpack," Mary said. "The car's stuck in the ditch."

Over the sound of groans and complaints, William Laurel introduced himself to the others. "Listen, even if the car wasn't stuck, there's no way we'd make it to Aviemore tonight. The snow's too fierce."

Hailey's mouth was pressed into a thin line, and Liz looked furious. Mary put her hand on her friend's arm.

"I know it's a nightmare, but honestly, the roads aren't safe. We just have to hang tight for now."

"It's not that. There's no bloody orange juice left, no mixers and only gin. Which I can't drink. And we're nearly out of frozen pizza." Liz pinched the bridge of her nose.

"I brought some supplies in the car," William said. "Nothing fancy, but some loaves of bread out of my freezer and some tins of beans. It'll keep us going until tomorrow."

"Tell me you at least brought some hot sauce?" Liz asked.

"Um... no," William said, edging back a little. "Is that a problem?"

Before Liz could speak, Bernie gave her a piercing look. "I'd like to have a chat with the other members of the WWC, if you don't mind Mr Laurel. We need to have a think about what we're going to do next."

"All right. I'll get the supplies out of the car. I might have a tin of hot dogs somewhere, if that helps?"

While the other members of the hen-do were squabbling over the last of the gin, Bernie led Mary and Liz upstairs to her bedroom.

"First things first," Bernie said, "How did your interviews go with the rest of the group?"

69

"You were only gone a few hours," Liz said. "I've just managed to speak to Pru so far. I tried Nora but she told me to… well, she used some Cockney slang that I hadn't heard before but I can guess what she meant."

"All right. Have you at least managed to pin down each person's movements that night?"

Liz flicked through her notepad. "Yes. The three of us went to bed first, as you'll remember, around eleven. Next to go was Trystesse, although I've not talked to her to get the exact time yet. Viola and Hailey went up before two, then Nora and Pru were an hour later."

"Can you tell how long Viola had been dead?" Mary asked, trying not to think about the woman in the bed staring sightlessly at the ceiling. "By the time we found her in the morning, I mean?"

Bernie shook her head. "Not really. You would need a doctor or a pathologist for that. I can only tell you that the body was cold and stiff, so that probably means she had been dead for more than an hour, but I couldn't say exactly."

"Then she was killed sometime after she went up to bed at two but before six-thirty in the morning."

"Probably earlier than that," Bernie said. "I was awake by six, so I would have heard someone moving about then."

Mary rubbed her eyes. It had been a long day and it wasn't even getting dark yet.

Liz placed a hand on her bump. "So when Viola was

70

murdered, every other member of the hen party should have been in their beds, asleep."

"But someone wasn't," Mary said, unable to keep from shuddering.

"Exactly. Who was bunking up with who again?"

"You and Viola were in rooms by yourselves," Liz said. "Hailey was with Trystesse, Pru and Nora in another room, and Mary and I were in together."

Bernie straightened her pillow. "In theory that could mean that anyone sharing a room has an alibi. But the amount people were drinking, I'm not convinced that someone couldn't have snuck out of one of the twin rooms without being noticed."

"If only one of us had heard something. I sleep like the dead at the moment," Liz said, wincing at her own word choice. "Neither of you heard a thing?"

"I put my cookie monster eye mask on and I'm out like a light," Mary admitted.

"And I can sleep anywhere and through anything," Bernie said. "But we should make sure to ask the others if they heard anything, or noticed anyone out of bed. The only problem is they might cover for each other."

"Surely not. Not for a murderer."

"Maybe they were in it together," Bernie said. "There's something about this whole situation that feels a bit too good to be true. A cottage in the middle of nowhere, no phones, no internet…. Perfect place for a murder."

"You're thinking of Hailey, aren't you?" Mary asked.

"She planned the hen-do. Booked everything. It makes sense."

"We should talk to her next," Bernie said.

"I'll do it," Liz said. "She might respond better to me than to you?"

"Why?" Bernie looked affronted.

"She described you as 'the nurse with the stick up her arse'. She doesn't like me much, but she likes you even less."

"Fair enough," Bernie shrugged. "We'll have to talk to them all today at some point."

"Why don't I chat to Trystesse?" Mary said, thinking of the quiet girl in the corner.

"Why? Because you're scared of the others?"

"What? No!" Mary tried to laugh but it just came out in a kind of strangled squeak. Liz just looked at her. "Okay, maybe I find them a little bit intimidating. Like the film *Mean Girls*, only they're bigger and taller and I'm trapped in a house with them and one of them is a psycho murderer."

"Well, when you put it that way, maybe you better stick with the quiet farm girl," Bernie said. "Liz and I can handle the others."

Five minutes later, Mary found Trystesse sitting in the conservatory staring out at the snow.

"Hi."

The woman looked up at her. "Is it my turn for the interview?"

"Yes, if that's all right." Mary wrapped her arms around herself. "It's chilly in here, isn't it?"

"The grumpy old farmer turned the thermostat down. Hailey said he was muttering something about 'women not putting jumpers on'. Still, it feels better having him in the house."

"I'm so sorry about your cousin," Mary said.

"Funny, you're the first person to say that to me. Hailey was right, you are the nice one."

Mary almost laughed. "They've been talking about me, have they?"

"All three of you. They don't like you much. Hailey was saying you would be poking your noses into our business. That you were a group of dowdy busybodies without a fashion sense between you. Sorry," Trystesse added, realising belatedly that she was repeating an insult.

"That's okay. Do you agree with Hailey?"

"Oh no. I think your 'Free Britney' t-shirt is kind of cute."

"Actually, it's Free Bert n' Ernie. Um, it's meant to be a pun. Anyway, it doesn't matter."

"Right. Well, if you ask me, anything you can find out that helps catch whoever killed Viola is a good thing."

"And you're not worried about us 'poking around in your business'?"

"I'm afraid I'm terribly boring. I work on my parent's farm, I don't go out much. I spend my nights reading books and watching telly. That sort of thing. Not like those women in the kitchen. They're much more exciting. Even Viola wasn't much compared to them, working in the school. In fact…"

"What?"

"Well, it's funny, if anyone was going to be murdered, then I would have thought it would be Hailey."

"Hailey? Why?"

"You could tell that only Viola really liked her. The other two, Pru and Nora, they weren't even pretending to get on with her. I mean, they didn't like me either, obviously, but I wasn't a threat to them."

"A threat? Why would Hailey be a threat?"

Trystesse bit her lip. "Maybe that's too strong a word. But, I guess it was like… well, Viola, Pru and Nora were a group."

"Like *Mean Girls*."

"Exactly!" Trystesse smiled. "And then when Hailey came along, it sort of upset the whole dynamic. And then once everyone started drinking, well, it all came out."

"It did?"

"Yeah. Pru was mad that Hailey was the bridesmaid, not her."

Mary leaned forward. "Is that so?"

"Yeah. There was a bit of name calling. It started getting nasty, so I went up to bed."

"Did you hear anything else? I mean, I wouldn't say that not being made a bridesmaid was a motive for murder."

Trystesse looked down at her feet. "No, it isn't. But that's the problem. Why would anyone kill my cousin? She wasn't perfect, but she wasn't bad enough for anyone to want her dead."

Mary couldn't think of anything to say. She could hear the drip of water on the conservatory roof. Did that mean that the snow was starting to thaw?

"They'll be missing you at home," she said, just for something to say. To Mary's astonishment, the other woman burst into tears.

"Sorry," Trystesse said, pulling a well-used wad of tissues out of her sleeve. "It's just, I'm so worried about the farm. The lambs will be coming, and all this snow... Those women in there, with their city lives, they don't have a clue what it's like for me and Paul. If we lose the lambs we might lose half our income for the year."

Mary reached over and squeezed her hand. "I'm sure we'll get out of here soon."

"We better. I never wanted to come on this stupid trip anyway. Viola said she needed me there, she said she –" Trystesse pressed her lips together, like she was stopping the words from coming out.

"What did she say?" Mary prompted.

"Nothing. Just that she wanted the best hen-do ever. And look how that worked out for her."

Trystesse disappeared behind her mound of tissues, but for the first time, Mary wasn't fooled. The woman was hiding something.

Chapter 10: Liz

Liz had spent so much of the day silently counting to ten, it was like she was an accountant again. It was partly the hormones, of course, that were making her tetchy. And the fact that her back ached from carrying around a watermelon on her stomach. But mainly what was making her grind her teeth were her fellow hens.

"Beans on toast. Not exactly Instagrammable is it," Nora said, poking her fork into her dinner.

If she was honest, Liz wasn't loving the food either, but she shovelled down the beans and soggy bread without complaint. The baby needed fed, and at least beans were one of your five-a-day. Mind you, she could have garrotted someone for some hot sauce.

Trystesse had taken her dinner up to her room. Liz wondered if anything had gone on in the interview with Mary, but she hadn't had a chance to ask. Part of the problem with investigating Viola's murder was that it was impossible to ever be somewhere you might not be overheard.

Bernie was at the kitchen counter, helping the farmer rustle up the food.

Liz pulled her tired body out of her chair and walked over to her friend.

"I'm making a crudité plate," Bernie explained.

"It seems to be mainly carrots. Or, in fact, entirely carrots."

"That's all we've got. But I did find an out-of-date tin of salsa in the cupboard, so we have a dip. We all need to keep our anti-oxidants up."

"Great," Liz said, trying for enthusiasm but with some sarcasm making its way out. "What's the plan for tonight?"

"William is going to try and get the car the right way up, for a start."

The man grimaced. "I've found some chains out back, and I'm going to give it a try."

He didn't seem very hopeful, and Liz didn't push the subject. Surely the weather would improve overnight and they would be able to get out tomorrow. She didn't know how much longer she could stand being in this place.

"Right, that's it." Hailey stormed into the kitchen, her eyes narrowed. "Someone has to own up, right now."

Liz raised her eyebrows it was a novel way of trying to find out who the murderer was. Like in school when you had to put your hand up if you were the one that nicked Penny Brown's yoghurt.

"I'm not leaving this room until someone owns up," Hailey said. Her left eye was twitching and Liz wondered if she had gone back on the gin.

"What are you talking about?" Pru asked.

78

"My phone. Someone's nicked it out of my room when I was charging it."

No one looked Hailey in the eye, but it was clear what they were thinking. The woman had lost the plot. Probably from the strain of the murder, although she had been coping all right up until now.

"Why would anyone take your phone?" Pru said in a bored-sounding voice. "They don't even work right now?"

"I don't know, but I've looked all over the place."

Something occurred to Liz and she turned and whispered to Bernie. "Was Viola's phone in her room?"

Bernie blinked. "I'm not sure. I didn't see it."

"What are you two saying?" Hailey said, striding towards them. "If you lot have nicked my phone I will slap you back home to Invergryff."

"Of course we haven't taken your phone," Bernie said. "Although, if we had, what do you think we would find on it?"

"Nothing!" Hailey's cheeks were turning red. "What exactly are you implying?"

Bernie chopped the carrot into finger-length slices. "It's quite simple. If someone took your phone, they did it for a reason. There must be something on it worth stealing."

"Or someone saw a chance to make a quick buck. It was the latest model, worth the best part of a grand."

"A grand!" Mary looked appalled. "Do people spend a grand on a phone?"

"Is anyone else missing their phones?" Liz asked. The others checked their pockets, but eventually everyone shook their heads.

"Why don't I have a look through all your suitcases then," Hailey said. "The phone's got to be in one of them."

"You can try it," Nora said, her lips a thin line.

Liz swallowed. She didn't like how this was going. She was pretty sure Bernie, Mary and her could stop a fight, but it wouldn't exactly be great for morale. Especially while they were still trapped in the middle of nowhere.

"Look, we're going to be going to the police station first thing tomorrow. We'll tell them about your phone when we explain about Viola's death. I'm sure they will do a full search then."

Hailey stomped away to keep searching the house.

"We should interview her now," Bernie whispered to Liz.

"She's already annoyed with us. Wouldn't it be better to wait?"

"She's on edge. Now is the perfect time. Take Mary with you. I want to see how the others get on without Chief Bridesmaid around to boss them about."

Liz sighed, but moved towards the door. It was better to be doing something, at least, than sitting about waiting. And even though the nurse often drove her mad, Liz was happy to have

Bernie back at the cottage. It felt safer, somehow. And at least she would force them to eat some vegetables.

Having collected Mary, Liz asked Hailey to come with them to the living room, which had somehow become their interview room of choice.

"I still think you should be spending your time getting us out of here, not asking silly questions," Hailey said with a sniff, but she did sit down on the sofa without further complaint.

"We thought it was important to speak to the person that organised everything," Liz said.

"You did such a good job," Mary added. Liz thought this was laying it on a little thick, particularly given the presence of the corpse in the garage, but Hailey gave them a tight little smile.

"Thanks. I don't think anyone else realises how much work these things are. Booking everyone, getting the deposits sorted... all while I could be doing other things. I actually have a very busy job, you know."

"You're a solicitor, is that right?"

"Yes. Look, I know fine well that legally speaking I have no reason whatsoever to talk to you two."

Liz and Mary exchanged a worried glance.

"Then you're not going to answer our questions?" Liz asked.

"Oh, I'll answer them. But only if you do something for me."

Liz had a feeling she knew what was coming next. "You want

81

us to find your phone?"

Hailey grinned. "Bingo. I want you to search everyone's suitcases. You have a perfect excuse for sneaking around, and I need that phone back."

"Fine," Liz said, knowing that she was creating an issue for herself in the future, but not really minding. It might be quite a good idea anyway to have a poke around in the other hens' suitcases and see if anyone was hiding anything.

Hailey leaned back on the sofa. "What do you want to know?"

Liz looked at her notes. "Tell me why you chose this cottage?"

"Viola wanted something out of the way. She said she didn't want everyone to sit on their phones all day. So I looked for somewhere in the middle of nowhere. Of course, I wish I hadn't ended up with somewhere quite so remote."

Liz wondered if it had really been Viola's choice to come somewhere so isolated. They only had Hailey's word for it, after all.

"And you didn't see or hear anything after you went to bed last night."

"You're joking, right? Trystesse was snoring before I even put the light out. I put the white noise app on my phone and put in my headphones. Didn't wake up until breakfast time, and then, well, I was with you lot when we found the... poor bloody Viola. No one even seems that bothered that she's dead, just annoyed that she's ruined their weekend."

Liz looked down at her feet, even though that was kind of hard to do at the moment. Truth be told, she had never been that big a fan of Viola. The woman was funny, but in that kind of harsh way where it was always other people that were the butt of the jokes.

"How did you two become friends?" Mary asked.

"We met through Alfie, actually, not long after they started going out. Alfie's dad was one of my clients, and Alfie came along to a Christmas party at my work with Viola. I think Viola was kind of bored, you know. Alfie's dad is one of those Alan Sugar types, always wanting to talk business, and that wasn't really her thing."

"Didn't she study business at college?"

Hailey laughed. "Yeah, only because she wanted to be an 'influencer'. That didn't last long once she realised how much competition there was. I think that was what attracted her to Alfie in the first place."

"Alfie is an 'influencer'?" Liz said, saying the word awkwardly like it was in a foreign language.

"Yeah, he's all over social media. Promoting his dad's hotels and things. Viola loved all that stuff, the posh cars and things." Hailey sniffed. "I mean, I'm making her sound shallow, but it wasn't like that. She never had much money growing up so you can understand why she was so into the designer stuff. And she was generous too. Like, Alfie was always buying her nice bags and shoes and things, but half the time she didn't even like them. She would give them to me for nothing if she thought I might use them. Those bitches in there never saw that side of her."

"You mean Pru and Nora, I take it."

"Well, they're bad enough, but at least they're honest with it. It's Tryss that's the worst of all."

"Really?"

"Yeah, she was really narked with Viola last night. Going on about how she had 'forgotten her roots'. Pure jealousy, that's all it was."

Liz looked at Mary. "Do you think Tryss was angry enough to do something about it?"

Hailey shook her head. "Like murder her own cousin? No, I don't think so. And the same goes for those stuck-up Londoners as well. They might have talked about Viola behind her back, but why would anyone kill her?"

Liz sighed. "We have no idea. And that's the problem."

Chapter 11: Bernie

In the kitchen, William Laurel had disappeared to fiddle about with the Land Rover, and Bernie was left with an increasingly sorry-looking collection of hens. Without Hailey there, Tryss was too nervous to sit with the English girls, so she had pulled a chair over to the patio doors and was pretending to look at a magazine. Pru and Nora were whispering together at the dining table in front of plates of untouched baked beans. They hadn't even eaten the carrot sticks.

"I'm going to go and check on the car," Pru said, getting out of her seat. After a few moments, Tryss mumbled something and drifted out of the kitchen towards the stairs. That left Nora behind, looking rejected and reaching for her wine glass.

Bernie gave the woman a good stare. When Bernie had first met Nora she had been impressed by how immaculate the woman looked. It hadn't surprised her to learn that the woman owned a beauty salon. If her clients could see Nora right now, they might have been in for a surprise. Mascara had run down her cheeks and was stuck to her face. Her lips were chapped and her hair was tied back into a messy bun.

"You look dehydrated," Bernie said, walking over to the table. "You should drink some water."

"The gin is going down fine, thank you very much."

Bernie wondered if the woman was an alcoholic or merely drinking to forget about her friend's death. Either way, it was irresponsible. And foolish. It meant that Bernie would be able to question her without the woman being able to comprehend what she was being asked. The ideal suspect.

"We're asking everyone to give a statement about what happened last night."

"Playing at policemen, aren't you? Or policewomen?"

"I think they prefer to be called police officers these days," Bernie said.

"Is that right? Well, whatever they're called, you're not one of them. So why the hell should I talk to you?"

Bernie shrugged. She wasn't impressed by the woman's posturing. "There's no one else here. What are you going to do anyway? Drink more gin? Spend your time chatting to a murderer?"

Nora frowned. "What do you mean?"

"It's quite simple. Someone in this house killed Viola. Either you're the killer, and there's not much point in me questioning you as you won't tell me anything anyway. Or you're sharing a house with the killer. Just like I am. In which case, you should be doing everything you can to catch them."

The woman shrugged but didn't complain any further.

"Can you confirm the timeline that Pru gave us for Friday night? You were the last to go up to bed, is that correct?"

"Yes. Everyone else flaked out, so we kept chatting. We were pretty blitzed by that point. I don't know who brought the gin, but it was nasty cheap stuff. Tasted like petrol."

"I brought the gin," Bernie said.

Nora laughed. "Of course you did. Well, it might have been nasty, but we drank it anyway. By that point, we'd have drunk aftershave if it had been going."

"Have you always had an alcohol problem?"

"What? It's not a problem. It was just because we were having such a rubbish time."

Bernie sniffed. She was not convinced, but there was no point in pursuing it. "Did you notice anything unusual that night? Did Viola seem worried at all?"

To give the woman credit, she took her time before answering, like she was considering the question.

"I don't think so. I mean, it wasn't the best atmosphere. I could see that Viola was hoping for a bit more of a luxury hen-do than this place. We'd thought it would be like a proper spa retreat, you know? So everyone was a bit annoyed at Hailey. And then you lot went upstairs early, and Viola was annoyed about that too."

"But she didn't seem frightened of anything? Or anyone?"

"No. If she had thought that… that someone was going to attack her, I'm sure she would have said something."

"Maybe. But there were no fallouts with anyone?"

"Nah. Bit of bickering, nothing more."

"And you can't think of anything strange, anything that might give us a clue as to why someone might want to kill her?"

"Well… it's probably nothing, but there was something weird going on about Viola and money," Nora said.

Bernie nodded. "Liz told me that Viola had been lording it over the rest of you when she got together with her rich fiancé."

"No, not that. I mean, before then. When we were at college, Viola didn't have any spare cash. Then she started working in the school and all of a sudden she was minted. I didn't think schools paid very well."

"They don't," Bernie frowned. "Especially their secretaries. Did you have any idea where the money was coming from?"

"She never said. But she used to make little comments when I was setting up the business, like, only fools paid taxes and I should be more 'creative' with my accounting. The last thing I want is the HMRC breathing down my neck, so I just ignored her. But it did make me wonder if she had some sort of scam going on herself."

"She didn't seem like the sort of person to be conning HMRC," Bernie said.

Nora snorted a laugh. "Then you really didn't know her that well. She grew up poor, right? So did I, although not as bad as Viola. When you've experienced life with no money, you'll do anything to get your hands on some."

"But you don't know what exactly she was into?"

"No."

Nora picked a bit of old mascara off her cheek and flicked it onto the floor.

"It's funny that Viola picked Hailey to be her bridesmaid," Bernie said. "I mean, considering that you and Pru have been friends with her for longer."

The floor shook and Nora jumped to her feet. "What a lot of rubbish you talk. Do you really think I would kill my friend because she didn't make me her bridesmaid? Why would I give a crap?"

Thinking that she had touched a nerve, Bernie stayed where she was. "I heard that you were arguing about it last night."

"We were having a laugh about it, that's all. Hailey was born to be a bloody bridesmaid, she loves bossing everyone about. Let me guess, the little hillbilly told on us."

"You're referring to Trystesse, I assume?"

"Yes. She's even worse than you lot, looking down her nose on us. Just because we live in London and like a bit of makeup doesn't make us all bimbos and airheads."

"Is that what Trystesse thinks?"

"You think we haven't noticed the side-eye? Of course that's what she thinks. It makes her feel better about her sad little life. And as for you lot…"

"What?" Bernie asked. She was quite enjoying the woman's rant. It always revealed more about someone when they let their emotions run away with them.

"You think you're better than the rest of us, don't you?" Nora said.

"No. Just smarter."

Nora stood up. "That's it. I'm done. The most surprising thing about this weekend is that no one has murdered you, Bernie Paterson."

Chapter 12: Walker

It was nine o'clock on Saturday night, but Walker was still on his laptop. He had some training modules to complete for work, and he wanted to get a handle on them before he was in the office. It was a testament to how far he had come in the last year that when he loaded up the document and scrolled through the lines of text, he didn't feel the usual churning sensation in his stomach. Instead, he clicked on his text reader app and opened a packet of crisps while the words washed over him.

He would have to listen to it a few times, of course, and make notes, but he would get there. And really, it was Mary he had to thank for it. She had been so calm when he had told her about his dyslexia, and because her son had a diagnosis, she knew exactly the sort of things that would help. Walker felt a smile tug at his lips. From the outside, people might think that Mary Plunkett was an unsuitable choice of girlfriend for him, but in so many ways they just worked together.

He checked his phone. No messages.

There was no point worrying, Walker told himself as he closed the laptop and stared at the ceiling. The reception was bad up north, that was all.

He reached for the remote and clicked on the television. The twenty-four hour news scrolled by in its usual dirge of misery, but Walker was thinking about a woman in Doc Martens and a print dress covered in Siamese cats. It was a horrible dress, he thought, and no one else on earth would be able to pull it off, but somehow she did. Mary had worn it on their first proper date, one that hadn't involved anyone being murdered. They had gone to an Italian restaurant overlooking the Abbey. A five o'clock dinner, of course, as she had had to be home for bedtime. But those two hours had been something special. There had been girlfriends before, and some relatively serious ones, but he had never clicked so quickly with someone. Mary had spent the whole time laughing, which he was almost sure was a good thing. And they hadn't looked back from there.

Some pictures of snow-covered roads appeared onscreen, and Walker's attention gradually drifted towards the telly.

"A storm front from the west has combined with the unseasonably cold weather to produce a snowstorm in the cairngorms. The A9 has been closed since yesterday and local residents are advised to remain at home."

A crease appeared between Walker's eyebrows as he watched.

"Some rural parts of the region are completely inaccessible, and there have been widespread reports of power outages. Farmers in the region are particularly concerned about the effect on the lambing season –"

He clicked off the television and sat in silence. There was positively, absolutely, definitely nothing to worry about.

No messages. Walker pulled up the maps app on his phone. If the A9 was shut, there wasn't much of an alternative, unless you went round by Braemar and Tomintoul, but that would add several hours to the journey.

Not that he was going anywhere, of course. Even if the power went out, they would be perfectly fine. It might mean the hot tub was out of bounds, but nothing more serious than that. After all, people in the Highlands were used to this sort of thing. And it was only for a couple of days. Probably.

Someone rang the doorbell. Walker got up, surprised, and looked out of the window. Standing outside was Liz Okoro's husband, Dave.

He hurried to the door to let the man in.

"Something wrong?" Walker asked. He had never seen the point in small talk, and Dave wasn't a close enough friend to just turn up without warning.

"No, nothing really. I probably shouldn't have come. Only… have you seen the weather forecast?"

Walker nodded. "I was just watching the news. Do you want to come in?"

"No. I've got Sean in the car. I just wanted to check that you hadn't heard anything. You know, through your work. I just keep thinking if they were driving on those roads, late at night… Anything might have happened."

"I haven't heard anything," Walker said in his most reassuring voice. Dave was an optician, and Walker had only ever seen him in the guise of confident father and laid-back bloke. Now he was twisting on his feet, his shoulders high and his fists clenching and unclenching.

93

"You're going to tell me that I'm worrying about nothing," the man said, managing a lopsided smile. "I know I'm being a fool about all this."

"Actually, I'm not," Walker said.

Dave's eyes widened. "Then what do we do about it?"

"We don't do anything," Walker said firmly. "But I'm going to do something. If we don't hear anything tonight, I'm going to go up there first thing tomorrow morning."

The other man's shoulders relaxed a little. "That would be great. How are you going to get there through the snow?"

"I'll work that out tonight. Leave it in my hands, okay?"

"Sure. I'll owe you a few beers for this one."

Walker watched the man walk back to his car, glad to see that he seemed a bit calmer. Once Dave had left, Walker closed the door and leaned against it with his eyes shut. He hadn't realised that he was going to Aviemore until he had announced it to the other man, but now it was the only thing he could think about. Was it an overreaction? Probably. But it was infinitely better than staying at home and doing nothing but checking his phone every five minutes.

He started to make some calls.

Chapter 13: Mary

Mary walked into the kitchen at ten o'clock to find that Liz and Bernie seemed to be the only people about.

"Where is everyone?"

Liz stifled a yawn. "Most of the women are in the living room, I think. Someone found the old DVD collection and they were going to put on *Pretty Woman*. No one seemed that up for it, but no one wanted to go upstairs either. Killer or no killer, I'm going to have to go to bed soon, if Bernie will stop pestering me about spreadsheets."

"Excuse me for wanting to catch a murder," Bernie grumbled.

"Well, I'm not sure I can add much to the spreadsheets," Mary said. "I tried to catch Trystesse again to see if she would tell me anything else, but she just made evasive comments and ran off to find Hailey. I'm sure she's hiding something." Mary felt frazzled. She hadn't managed to contribute much to the investigation, and she was sure Bernie thought that she wasn't pulling her weight. There was also the nagging worry that the kids might be trying to get in touch with her, but she couldn't see any of their messages.

"We need to search the bedrooms," Bernie said, glancing at Liz. "Are you sure all the women are in the living room together?"

"Last I looked," Liz said. "The farmer is still trying to connect some sort of old radio out in the shed. I have no idea why. It's not like he'll be able to contact anyone with it."

"Men like to feel useful," Bernie said. "And I'm quite happy to have him out of the way. It means we can continue our investigations in peace."

Mary nodded. "We did say to Hailey that we would look for her phone. I've had a good look around the kitchen, but it doesn't seem to be there. I even went back through the bags of rubbish and recycling. You wouldn't believe how many bottles of booze we've gotten through."

"I would believe it," Bernie said primly, "I saw the state of you lot last night."

Mary pouted. "I wasn't that bad."

"Did you start doing karaoke?"

A flash of singing Britney Spears complete with dance moves streaked across Mary's consciousness. "No, I'm sure that was someone else. So how are we going to search these rooms without anyone catching us?"

"I'll be the lookout," Bernie said, suspiciously quickly.

"It won't be you that gets caught grubbing around in someone's undie drawer, then," Liz groaned. "Why is it always us that have to do the dirty work?"

"Because I'm a better lookout. Mary always gets distracted by her stomach, and you're always on your phone checking the stock market."

Both Mary and Liz shrugged at this. They couldn't deny it.

"Go upstairs, start with Hailey and Trystess's room and search them all," Bernie said, practically shoving them towards the stairs. "And don't just look for a signed confession. Make a note of any weird stuff you come across, anything that seems out of place. There's got to be some sort of clue to what happened, even if we don't realise how significant it is yet."

"All right," Mary said, although she wasn't happy about it. She had a feeling that the cool kids would never let her into their gang if they caught her looking through their stuff.

"You can count on us," Liz said, speaking around another yawn.

Bernie rolled her eyes, then plonked herself down on the stairs with an old trashy magazine that she had rustled up from somewhere.

"Will you hoot like an owl when they're coming," Mary whispered as she walked up the stairs.

"No. I'll shout to you that the tea's ready. That's the signal."

Mary nodded, even though she was disappointed. It seemed like poor spycraft. They could have at least imitated a bird call, or maybe even a wolf howl.

By the time Mary had climbed the stairs, Liz had already opened the door to Hailey and Trystesse's room. Slipping inside and shutting the door behind her, Mary felt the hairs on the back of her neck stand on end. She looked over to Liz whose unhappy expression mirrored her own.

97

"Let's just do this as quickly as we can and get out," Liz said and Mary was in full agreement.

The two sides of the twin bedroom were clearly occupied by two very different people. On Hailey's side, nothing was out of place, even down to the pyjamas folded neatly on the pillow. Mary, one of life's inherently messy people, wondered if there was something odd about being so tidy when your best friend had just been murdered. She felt much more empathy with Trystesse, who hadn't even bothered to make her bed. Her side of the bed was strewn with clothes, books and toiletries as if a hurricane had passed through.

"I'll take Trystesse, you do Hailey," Liz whispered and they got to work.

"Sure." First Mary checked under the mattress. If life was anything like a good detective story, there would be something hidden in there, but there was nothing. Hailey was the sort of person who actually removed her clothes from the suitcase and put them in the drawers, so Mary tackled them next.

Mary checked everything including the socks, but there was nothing hidden. There was – disappointingly – no diary detailing how Hailey had murdered her best friend. In fact, the closest thing was a Filofax type thing with work meetings listed. Mary took pictures of the last few weeks, just in case it proved important.

"Jesus, Trystesse was messy," Liz said, keeping her voice low. "I've just found a chocolate bar wrapper stuck to one of her slippers. I'm nearly done here, how about you?"

"Not much left. You know, I feel pretty gross looking through all this stuff," Mary said.

Liz nodded. "Me too. But we don't have another choice. I know Bernie sees things in black and white, but this is one of those times that she's right. There's a murderer here, and we need to find them."

Mary sighed and kept going through the drawers. Deep down, she agreed with the others, but that didn't mean she was happy about it.

"What do we do if we find any evidence? Like, if there's a bloody knife in the next drawer, are we going to have a confrontation with Hailey? Or do we pretend that everything is fine?"

"I don't think we're going to find a bloody knife. Mainly because Viola wasn't stabbed."

"But you see my point. We're not the police, we can't arrest anyone, so…"

"We'll cross that bridge when we come to it," Liz said, in a tone that ended the discussion. "Let's move on to Pru and Nora's room.

They crossed the hallway to the other twin room. Nora and Pru were both relatively tidy, although there were two empty wine bottles on top of the chest of drawers, and the room smelled like a bag hangover.

Liz walked over to Nora's side of the room and started to work her way through the tremendous collection of beauty products.

Pru's handbag was sitting on the bed. Mary undid the clasp and had a look inside. It had the usual jumble of makeup, tissues and other detritus, but there were also some letters. Mary's eye was drawn to an official-looking piece of paper that looked like it had been folded and refolded several times. She took it out and read it.

"Liz, take a look at this. Does it mean what I think it does?"

Liz looked over Mary's shoulder to read the letter. "Oh wow, her HR business is in serious trouble. This is a letter from her lawyers. It's basically saying that if they don't improve cash flow in the next few weeks, the whole company is going to go into administration."

"I'm guessing Pru didn't mention that in her interview."

"She certainly did not. She painted herself as quite the successful businesswoman. According to this, she needs to find half a million quid, and she needs to do it soon."

"Did Viola have that sort of money? Could it be a motive for murder?"

Liz frowned. "I don't see how. Killing Viola doesn't mean that you would get her money. Even if she had that sort of cash, it would all go to her next of kin, wouldn't it?"

"You would think so," Mary replied. She took out her phone and snapped a photo of the letter before carefully placing it back into Pru's handbag.

An expert now at conducting illicit searches, it didn't take her long to finish Pru's side of the room. Liz looked up from the final drawer on Nora's side and gave her a weak smile.

"Let's get out of here. We should take a final look at the bathrooms, then we can call it a day."

Relieved, Mary moved into the bathroom. There were a few washbags and toothbrushes scattered around and she rifled through their contents without noticing anything interesting. Trystesse had a packet of anti-depressants in her washbag, but Mary didn't think that was particularly note-worthy. Last of all, she had a look in the bin, which was gross but necessary. There was nothing in there either. But when she went to put the bin back she noticed a silver packet behind it. She picked it up, then went to get her friend.

"You left your pregnancy vitamins in the bathroom," Mary said when she found Liz in one of the en-suites. "They slipped down behind the bin."

Liz walked over and stared at the packet. "Those aren't mine."

"What?"

"They're not mine. I've got a different brand, and besides I've never used this bathroom."

Mary put her hand to her mouth. "Please tell me they couldn't have been Viola's!" The thought was too awful.

Liz shook her head. "I don't think so. Viola had an en-suite, remember. Besides, she told me that they had decided to wait until they were married to have kids because she wanted to stay 'bikini ready' for the honeymoon."

Relieved, Mary turned the packet over in her hands. "There's no sign of whose it could be. But we know that Pru and Nora were using this bathroom."

"Both of them have been drinking like fishes," Liz said in a disapproving voice.

"Or pretending to," Mary said thoughtfully, "I mean, it's not that hard to pretend to be drunk when everyone else is. It could be Trystesse or Hailey's too. Even though they had their own bathroom, they could have come in here. There's no way of ruling them out."

"It doesn't have to be relevant, of course," Liz said. "They might be in the early stages and not wanting to tell anyone yet. Still, let's add it to the list of 'weird stuff' for Bernie."

Chapter 14: Liz

It took them until after nine o'clock on Saturday night to finish the search. Luckily, the other women were so engrossed in whether or not the beautiful prostitute would hook up with the creepy businessman, they never ventured upstairs. Liz was exhausted. Once they collected Bernie and went downstairs, she started thinking up reasons to go to bed. Had it only been this morning that they had discovered one of their friends was dead? This Saturday would go down in history as the longest day Liz Okoro had ever experienced.

"You look dreadful," Bernie said, coming over to her with a Tupperware tub. "Have a protein ball, it'll be good for the baby."

Liz popped one of the dark grey balls into her mouth. Instant regret. "What the hell is in this," she said, struggling to get the words out as the stuff coated her tongue.

"Peanut butter, chia seeds, goji berries, agave nectar and flax."

"Mmn," Liz managed, while Mary mimed puking at her behind Bernie's back.

The other women came in a few moments later.

"Couldn't concentrate," Hailey explained, opening the fridge and pulling out another bottle of cheap booze.

Trystesse and Nora slumped onto the dining chairs. Half the

women in the kitchen looked like they were asleep already. Either that, or they were buzzing with leftover adrenaline, like Pru who was pacing up and down in front of the patio doors.

"I think the snow might be easing," she said. "Do you think the farmer might try another trip out tonight?"

"Not now it's dark," Bernie replied. "He's gone out to the car again, but it's still stuck fast. Last I saw he was poking about in the shed looking for tools, but he didn't seem very optimistic."

"I thought farmers were meant to be knowledgeable about these things. How the hell has he ended up in a situation where he can't get off the farm and we're stuck here?" Pru said.

"He can't do anything about the weather," Trystesse replied.

"Well, I guess you would know, wouldn't you? You're a farmer's wife, isn't that right?"

Trystesse gave the other woman a tight-lipped smile. "I suppose so. It's a smallholding really, rather than a farm. We call it a croft, although it's a bit small, even for that. We have a little farm shop, though, on the road to Pitlochry, and that brings in some money…" She trailed off when she realised that Pru had stopped listening and gone back to pacing across the floor.

Even without the murder, these women would never have got on, Liz thought. The London girls, the rural cousin, the lawyer, and the three… what? Busybodies from Invergryff. If anything, Viola's death had given them something in common.

Liz grimaced. That was Bernie Paterson thinking. She needed to get out of this cottage and back to Dave and Sean. If she stayed much longer she would start enjoying the protein balls, and then there would be no hope for her whatsoever.

A beeping noise went off and Hailey touched her watch. "Cocktails at the hotel on the hill," she said. "That's what we should have been doing right now. Viola would have loved them. Then we were going to go to the karaoke bar."

"Well, that's a mercy at least," Bernie said.

It only took a second for Hailey to launch herself at the nurse. The woman's scream pierced the air as she jumped on Liz's friend.

"Get off," Bernie yelled, just as Hailey cracked her one to the jaw.

"Ow!"

Hailey jumped back, rubbing her hand. She looked as shocked as everyone else at what had happened. For a moment Liz thought she was going to apologise, then she got up to her feet and walked out of the room.

Liz went into the freezer and rooted around until she found a packet of peas. She walked back to Bernie who was now sitting on a chair, rubbing her chin.

"Here you go," Liz said, and Bernie held the peas up to her jaw.

"Didn't think she had it in her," Bernie said. "I didn't see either of you two rushing to pull her off me."

Liz caught Mary's eye, and the other woman shrugged.

"I think we probably felt that you deserved it. You were being particularly insensitive, even for you."

"I suppose I was," Bernie said, the trace of a smile on her lips. "But we learned something, didn't we? Hailey is happy to resort to violence when someone pushes her."

"I'm not sure about that," Liz said. "If anything it makes her less likely to commit the murder. Whoever killed Viola waited until everyone was asleep, then smothered her. It wasn't exactly a moment of rage. It was calculated, cold even."

"Whereas Hailey was volatile and emotional. I still feel a little put out that my fellow WWC members didn't come to my aid."

"I didn't want to get blood on my Tardis sweatshirt," Mary said.

"We should be banding together, not attacking each other," Trystesse said, her eyes watery.

"I don't know," Nora said, "that was the best entertainment we've had all evening. Better than a romcom any day."

Bernie was about to snipe back, when there was a noise that stopped her in her tracks.

Liz stood up. "What that…"

It happened again. It was a knock at the front door.

For a second no one moved, then Pru jumped to her feet. "Bloody hell, someone's made it!"

She ran to the door, and Liz and the others followed behind. Mary peeked out through the frosted glass next to the door.

"Look, it's a cop!"

"Oh thank god!"

The women gathered around.

"Let him in!"

Hailey had appeared from upstairs, strop forgotten and she pulled the door wide open to show the man in uniform standing outside. The police officer was young and male with a surprisingly orange kind of fake tan.

"Officer Pantsov. I take it this is the hen party?"

"Right, well it's about time you turned up," Hailey said. "It's been a bloody nightmare here without you."

"I got stuck in that snow for hours," he said. "I've only just made it up the road from Nethybridge."

"Hang on," Liz said, staring at the young man, "I think we might have a misunderstanding here."

"No, no, I'm ready to get on with it," the man said, pulling off his coat. His police uniform underneath was surprisingly tight-fitting. "Where's the bride-to-be?"

"We... well, we put her in the garage?"

"The garage?" The young man looked surprised. "Well, if that's what floats your boat."

"I think we should tell you what happened to Viola…" Bernie began.

"What, she's not shy is she?" He started to flex his biceps and did something that Liz thought the youngsters would call twerking.

"Oh dear god," Mary said, covering her eyes.

"Officer Pantsov," Liz said. "Or Pants Off, I presume. What a dreadful pun."

"You're the stripper!" Hailey said as realisation finally dawned.

"That's right. I know I'm an hour late, but they've still not opened up the main road."

"How the hell did you get up here then?"

"I stay three miles down the track. My dad gave me a lift in his jeep. He's sat in it right now, as a matter of fact."

"Your dad?"

The lad blushed. "Oh, he won't be any bother. He's got a book to read while I do my stuff and then he'll give me a lift back again. It's a Jack Reacher one."

"Jesus," Bernie said. "We've a dead body in the garage and our best chance at salvation is a stripper."

Officer Pantsov's eyebrows climbed up his orange forehead.

"Dead body? Hang on, is there some joke I'm not getting here?"

"No joke," Liz said. "There's been a…" she found she couldn't quite say the word murder, not to this man whose police uniform was wipe-clean. "There was an accident. The bride-to-be died last night. We've not been able to get an ambulance or even the police out because of the snow."

"Oh my god!" Officer Pantsov held his hands to his mouth. "You're not joking, are you?"

"No. Now, please tell me you've a working phone on you."

The young man shook his head. "The mast's down. My dad used to work for the electric board. He reckons it won't be back up again until tomorrow."

He slumped against the wall. "I don't suppose you'll be wanting any entertainment tonight then. I've been practising my Tom Jones all week."

"I'm sure you would have been very good," Mary said, giving him a pat on the shoulder. "What's your real name anyway?"

"Kevin. Kevin Muir."

"Well, Kevin, why don't you go and get your dad to come in here? Maybe he's got some idea how we can all get out of here."

Whether it was the disappointment of a failed rescue, or the stripper's aftershave, but Liz felt a headache settle in at her temples.

109

"I'm going upstairs for a minute," she said.

"Would you like a –" Trystesse started to say.

"No, I would not like a cup of tea. If I drink any more tea this baby will be swimming the backstroke before it's born."

Liz stomped upstairs and slammed the bedroom door behind her. She had never felt claustrophobic before in her life, but she knew that with every hour she spent in this cottage, she was getting closer to throttling someone.

It was only twenty blissfully silent minutes later when someone knocked on her door.

"Can I come in?" Bernie asked.

"Sure," Liz grunted.

"It's all kicking off downstairs. Someone – and I'm not saying it was Mary Plunkett, but I'm not saying it wasn't the silly cow – thought it might be good for morale if the stripper did some of his act. I think it's Elvis at the moment, but it's hard to tell given all the spray cream involved."

"Oh god."

"Yeah. And that's the good news."

Liz felt her shoulders slump. "What's the bad news?"

"Well, you're not going to believe this," Bernie said.

Liz stared into the cold cup of tea that was sitting on her bedside table. It had been there since lunchtime. "At this point

I'll believe anything."

"The stripper's dad can't get the car started. Battery's gone. So they're stuck here too."

Liz took a deep breath, but it didn't help. "That means it's the dead body, the hens, the farmer, the stripper and his dad, all trapped in the house until the snow melts?"

"That's right. Fancy another cup of tea?"

Chapter 15: Bernie

There was a stripper, his dad and the farmer in the living room, sleeping on the floor. It felt like some sort of filthy joke, but Bernie wasn't really in the mood.

In truth, she was feeling frustrated. The snow was easing, and by some means or other, she was sure they would be able to escape the cottage in the morning, and the timing couldn't be worse. Of course, she wanted to get out of the place as badly as the rest of them, but she didn't want to leave until she had some idea of who had killed Viola, and why. It would be humiliating to turn up at the police station in Aviemore with no theories, after having been on the scene when the murder was committed. She was an investigator, after all. It would do the reputation of the Wronged Women's Co-operative no good if they arrived in Aviemore empty-handed.

Mary and Liz had reported back with the results of the searches. Bernie had been hoping for some sort of connection between the suspects and Viola's death, but they hadn't managed to find it. Some surprises had been uncovered. Bernie had no idea who was pregnant, but it meant there was at least one secret being kept in the cottage. And arguably more interesting was the revelation about Pru's financial problems. Half a million in debt and her company about to go under, that would lead anyone to do something desperate. Pru had just placed herself at the top of the suspect list. The only problem was that it didn't seem to benefit the woman financially if Viola died. Bernie was working on a theory that

Viola had lent Pru some money, but until they could do some further investigations, there was no proof of any of it.

"That's Liz off to bed," Mary said, coming back into the kitchen. Hailey and Trystesse had already left to go upstairs, and the men had settled down in the living room. The last time she walked past, Bernie had heard them arguing about Highland League football, which showed they were getting on just fine.

"I don't want to go while those two are still up," Bernie said, glancing at Pru and Nora.

Mary shrugged. "The problem is they are probably thinking the same thing. You could come in and bunk with me and Liz tonight if you don't want to be on your own?"

"I think I'll pass. I want to be able to keep watch on the others, and it's easier to do that if I have the freedom to sneak in and out."

"Just like the murderer did," Mary said.

"Yep."

"Will you at least lock your room?"

"Of course. And you do the same. Don't think that the pregnant whale is going to be leaping out of bed quickly enough to save you from the midnight smotherer."

"Please don't call them that."

"What? They smothered at midnight? I thought it was quite a

113

good name."

"I meant... never mind."

Mary yawned and Bernie propelled her towards the door.

"You get off to bed now," she said firmly. "You're no use to me anyway in this state."

Once Mary had gone upstairs with only the smallest of protests, Bernie set her sights on Pru and Nora.

"How are you two doing?" Bernie asked.

Nora sniffed. "Oh come on, like you care."

"I care in as much as we need to all pitch in together. Hopefully they'll get us out of here tomorrow but if they don't..."

The wine glass Pru was holding started to tremble. "You can't think we'll be stuck here any longer than tonight, surely."

Bernie, who had noticed that the snow was already started to thaw, tilted her head to one side. "Could be several more days. By which time we'll know who the murderer is."

"You will, will you?" Nora asked. If she was faking being drunk, she was doing a damn good job. "Doesn't seem like you've managed to find out who it was so far. What makes you think you'd get there even if we were stuck here for a month?"

Bernie leaned forward across the dining table. "Because I think that this was a crime of opportunity. The killer can't have

114

planned in advance for a freak weather event like this. They saw their chance to kill Viola and they took it. Unplanned. And that's the sort of killer that makes mistakes. The sort of killer that the guilt is slowly eating away at them, hour after hour. In a couple of days, they'll be a nervous wreck."

The other women said nothing.

"In fact," Bernie continued, "it might be best for the killer all around if they just admitted it now. A moment of madness, that's what it was. If they confessed now, then we could work out a story before the police came. Explain how they hadn't been of sound mind, how it had just happened, and they had regretted it ever since. They could be at peace."

Silence rang out through the kitchen. Then Nora started to laugh.

"Come on now. Did you really think that would work? I'm off to bed," she stood up and with one last sneering glance at Bernie, headed for the door.

"You're looking in the wrong place, you know that?" Pru said.

"Tell me where the right place is, then," Bernie told her.

"Well… it might be nothing, but I know that there was some weird legal stuff going on between Hailey and Viola. I think Viola was getting her advice on something."

"How do you know this?"

"I overheard them on the train. They were queueing for the loo, then they saw me and shut up. Look, it might be nothing, but all I'm saying is there's plenty of people with something to hide in the cottage and it's not me and Nora."

"Is that it? They were talking about 'something legal'? Come on, if there's anything you want to tell me, now's the time to do it," Bernie said to Pru, as she too got up onto her feet.

"I've told you everything I know. Do you ever stop pushing people? Man, you are nuts," the other woman said. "You're more likely to be a murderer than anyone. Totally nuts."

With that, she followed her friend upstairs. Bernie got up to make herself a strong coffee. She hadn't really expected either of them to confess, but she wanted to shake them up a little. At least there was the hint of some 'legal stuff' between Hailey and Viola, so that was worth investigating. And Pru and Nora now knew that Bernie wasn't letting up on her questions, no matter how much they tried to fob her off.

Plus, their little flounce meant that everyone was now in their rooms and Bernie could prepare for the night ahead. Despite what she had told Mary and Liz, she was worried. As the boss of the WWC, she felt responsible for the lives of her colleagues, more than just as friends. The murderer had already made a fool of Bernie Paterson once by killing Viola right under her nose. She was not going to let that happen again.

Bernie did a circuit of the downstairs. The men had fallen asleep in the living room, snoring away happily. The patio doors and the front door were both locked. She checked twice, even though she knew the threat was inside, not out in the woods.

116

Next, she grabbed her cup of coffee and headed upstairs. Despite what Mary might think, she wasn't disturbed by the single room. It gave her a chance to stay up all night without anyone caring. And that was the plan, after all. No murderer was getting past her two nights in a row.

She turned on her laptop and worked on the spreadsheet. She had individual entries now for all the hens, but the motive column was still looking rather sparse.

Bernie was just thinking about another coffee when she heard a creak. Someone was going down the stairs. Quick as a flash, she was out of her bed. By the time she got to the stairs, however, they were gone. Was that a draft from the kitchen?

She had just walked towards the kitchen door when there was another creak from the floorboards upstairs. Someone was going to kill her friends! In a moment, Bernie was back up the stairs, just as Mary came out of the loo.

"Blast!" Bernie said.

Mary looked at her in confusion.

"Don't move," she said, and then she went to the other rooms and opened and shut each door. Every single person was accounted for.

"I don't understand," Bernie said slowly. "I heard someone on the stairs. They can't be... Damnit, they must have been coming back up the stairs, not going down them. What a fool I am."

"Maybe they just wanted a glass of water or something," Mary said.

"And then pretended to be asleep when I looked in? No, they were up to something, that's for sure. They won't try anything else now that they know we're up and about."

Mary rubbed her eyes. She was wearing a fluffy onesie that made her look like a yeti. "Does that mean it's safe for me to go back to bed?"

Bernie opened her mouth for a second, then closed it. Then she said quietly. "Of course. You should try and get some sleep."

The other woman nodded. "All right," she yawned. "I'll see you in the morning."

Bernie watched her friend go back into her room and close the door. Then she walked around the upstairs, opening each bedroom door as quietly as she could for the second time. Each member of the hen party was in their beds and sleeping soundly.

She made her way back downstairs and checked that the front door was still locked. She peeked her head into the living room where the three men were snoring away happily. Then she went into the kitchen to the patio doors. She looked down at the puddle of water that had collected in front of them. The doors were slightly ajar, so she turned the key until they were securely locked.

Had someone left it open by accident? Or had it been deliberate?

Either way, someone had come in from outside. Bernie knew that if she had said as much to Mary the woman would be running around in a panic, imagining all sorts of mysterious enemies lurking in the woods. But Bernie had already thought it through. The simplest solution was often the most likely. The person who she had seen outside had been someone from the house, who went out and came back in from the patio doors.

But why would anyone go out into the snow at this time of night?

After a moment's thought, Bernie rummaged in the hall cupboard and came out with a small torch.

As quietly as she could, she unlocked the patio doors and slipped outside. As she had hoped, the footprints were still clear in the snow. Perhaps if she had been a police officer, she might have been able to match them to the shoes of the inhabitants of the cottage, but in the dark, all she could see were depressions with no definable markings. But that wasn't what she was out here for anyway. Placing her feet in the holes that the previous person had made, she walked out into the snow.

They hadn't gone far. The footprints stopped twenty feet from the house. Just in front of them was a small hole in the blanket of white. Bernie reached forward and rooted around.

Then she touched something. She withdrew her hand and looked at her prize. It was a mobile phone.

Chapter 16: Walker

Walker made it to Aviemore before seven in the morning. The first part of the drive up from the central belt had been easy enough. He hadn't even seen any snow until he had gone north of Stirling. It was only when he got to the Cairngorms that he found the A9 closed to traffic. There had been a landslip, compounded by the thaw, and it was going to take most of the day to clear it.

Luckily, he had phoned ahead and a squad car was waiting for him in a layby.

"The back road to Aviemore has been ploughed," Constable Karen MacDonald told him when he pulled up alongside her car. "You'll get through to the town if you take your time. DI Macleod said you were on a rescue mission?"

"Something like that."

"Need any help?"

Walker shook his head. A snowflake slipped down the neck of his coat and melted on his skin. "I have a friend who is going to help me out. But if I run into trouble I'll call you."

Back in his car, he followed the Constable's directions for the back road. Even though the snow was nowhere near as bad as it had been in the last few days, it was still a treacherous drive. Eventually, he spotted the sign that said: 'Highland Battlefront – Enter at your Own Risk'. He turned up the lane.

He nearly spun off at one sharp corner, which would have been frustrating given how far he had come, but he managed to get his car to crawl up the hill. He stopped outside a series of old barns that were in various states of repair verging from the modernised to the practically falling down.

There was also an old farmhouse and this was where he headed, his feet crunching on the melting snow.

He rang the bell, noting that it wasn't even eight in the morning yet. But Walker wasn't worried. Sergeant Evan Flood had always been the sort of guy to get up with the larks. He had been the oldest member of the regiment out in Basrah, by quite some way. Should have been at home happily retired, really, but had elected to stay on for one last tour.

Walker had asked him why one day.

"How old are you?" the man had asked him.

"Nineteen."

"Well, there you are. Nineteen, just joined the army, no clue what you're doing and they've sent you into the worst conflict we've seen for decades. No offence, lad, but you are just an expendable grunt."

"Uh, thanks?" Walker had tried to laugh it off, but the Sergeant wasn't smiling.

"Six weeks of training for this. Where did you do it again?"

"In Wales."

"Aye, in Wales, in the winter. Excellent training for fighting out in the desert in forty degree heat."

Walker shrugged. He didn't need to be told how unprepared they were.

"Anyway, I was sat in my office, all ready to retire and I looked at you young lads coming in, more time playing computer games than handling real weapons and I thought… well, I thought if I was out there with you then maybe a few less of you poor sods might die."

It hadn't exactly been the sort of moral-boosting pep talk that Walker had been looking for at the time, but it didn't take long before he came to appreciate that having the grumpy Sergeant Flood around was a hell of a lot better than being without him. Flood's experience, his ability to work under pressure, his general don't-take-any-crap attitude to the officers, all of it was invaluable. And there were a few too many times, a few properly scary times, that Walker knew he and his fellow men only survived due to Flood's quick thinking in combat situations.

Flood had retired right after the operation in Basrah to run his off-road vehicle tours, but he had always kept in touch. Mainly through borderline offensive jokes sent on social media. Walker had always known that he would be the sort of man to rely on in a crisis.

Flood opened the door. Despite the cold, he was wearing desert combat shorts and a polo shirt that was struggling to contain his rapidly expanding stomach.

"Shortbread! I got your email. Come on in."

Walker managed to conceal his wince at the old nickname and went into the house. Over a cup of steaming hot tea, he went over the problem with his old friend.

"And you've not heard a thing from any of them?"

"Phone reception is down and they don't appear to have wifi access. I wouldn't worry at all, if it wasn't for the weather and the fact that one of them is pregnant." Walker could sense himself trying to justify his actions all over again. Now that he was sitting in Flood's nice little kitchen with decorative plates hung on the walls, it seemed hard to recreate the sense of dread he had felt last night.

"You were right to come," Flood said firmly. "Bunch of civvies stuck out in the middle of nowhere, no idea about the Highland weather... What if they went out for a hike somewhere when it turned nasty?"

Walked swallowed. He hadn't even considered that one.

"We'll go and check up on them. Just in case. And it gives me an excuse to get Big Bertha out."

Walker grinned, his worry evaporating. "I hoped you might say that."

Chapter 17: Mary

Mary woke up late on Sunday, but not as late as Liz who was still starfished on the bed, snoring softly with one hand on her bump. She crept downstairs into the kitchen to find Bernie was by herself.

"The other women have gone to help Mr Laurel to get the car upright," Bernie said as she passed Mary a protein bar.

"Great," Mary said, ripping the bar open and eating it without much enthusiasm. No matter what Bernie said about them, she always thought they tasted like cardboard and old cheese.

"I found something last night in the snow." Bernie held up a freezer bag with a mobile phone inside.

"Is it Viola's?" Mary asked, remembering that they had never found their dead friend's phone.

"No, it's Hailey's."

Mary frowned. "Are you sure? I mean, why would anyone chuck Hailey's phone out into the snow? It doesn't make any sense."

"The screensaver is a picture of her and her pet beagle. And it does make sense if Hailey was the one that chucked it. The whole 'who's stolen my phone' scene could have all been an act. She realised that there was something incriminating on the phone and she needed to dispose of it."

"But what could be on her phone that could be that bad?"

"I don't know. But it's got to be something connected to Viola's murder."

"You really think that Hailey did it?" Mary asked.

Bernie held up three fingers. "She booked a cottage in the middle of nowhere for the hen-do, giving her the means to do it without being caught." She put down one finger. "She knew that Viola would be drinking and that gives her the opportunity for murder." Another finger went down. "And on this mobile I reckon we're going to find the motive." Bernie put down the final finger.

"I just think it's a bit of a strange thing for a lawyer to do. Wouldn't someone with that sort of legal background be able to pull off a murder where they wouldn't get caught?"

Bernie screwed up her face. "The problem is she reckons that's exactly what's going to happen. But I'm going to make sure that Viola's killer spends the rest of their lives in prison, whether it's Hailey or any of the others."

Mary was shocked to hear the tremor in Bernie's voice. It wasn't often that she got emotionally involved in their cases. Or in anything, in fact. She must have really liked Viola, Mary thought. Then a second possibility occurred to her: maybe Bernie was just really worried about being outsmarted by somebody, even if it was a murderer.

Liz came into the kitchen and groped for the kettle.

"I'm having a black coffee and if a single person makes a

comment about pregnancy and caffeine then I will shove this kettle up their –"

"Good sleep, was it?" Bernie asked sweetly.

Liz just glowered at her.

"Well, this might cheer you up," Bernie said, taking the plastic bag with the phone out of her pocket. She told Liz all about her visit outside in the night.

"Did you check the messages?" Liz asked.

"That's the big problem. It is password locked and I can't get into it. I think we might have to hand it over to the police," Bernie said. "You'll have to sweet talk Walker into giving me a look at it."

Mary felt a twinge of longing in her chest at the thought of her boyfriend. "I'm not sure he'll be allowed. It'll be the Aviemore police we'll be dealing with. He'll be a hundred miles away."

Bernie ignored her. "When we get a look at the messages I'm hoping there's something from Viola on it. Maybe Viola was threatening Hailey with something? It would explain why Viola's phone disappeared as well."

Liz had wandered over to the patio doors. "Is it wishful thinking or has the snow thawed a bit."

Mary went over to join her. "I think so. But it still looks pretty bad."

There was a chorus of voices and the other women came into

the kitchen.

"Put that kettle back on," Pru demanded. "It's bloody freezing out there."

"Did you fix the car?" Mary asked.

"No chance," Hailey replied, flinging herself into a chair. "I don't know why we bothered. That thing is completely stuck."

"My fingers are numb," Nora complained. "And all my acrylics have come off."

Trystesse merely reached for a cup of tea and gulped it down. "If I have to spend any more time with those princesses, I'm going to lose my mind," she whispered to Mary.

"Were they that bad?" she asked.

"They weren't pushing at all!"

Mary smiled in sympathy, even though she knew she would have been exactly the same. She was just about to grab another cuppa when she heard something.

"What the hell is that noise?" she asked. For a while now, a low rumbling had been nudging at her attention.

"Is it a car?" Bernie said, and as one the women rushed to the front door.

"I can't see anything yet," Hailey said when she had wrenched the door open.

"It's too loud to be a car," Liz said. "Maybe a helicopter?"

"Do you think they would airlift us to the police station?"

"I think that's pretty unlikely. Besides, no one even knows about the murder yet. It's probably just flying past."

They looked up at the sky but there wasn't anything there.

"What the hell?" Mr Laurel appeared, his face still smeared with oil from his attempts to get his car upright. "It sounds like a snowplough or something, but they can't make it up this road. The snow is too deep."

More excited by the mention of the word snowplough, the rest of the women pressed in behind Mary and the others.

"Can you see it yet?" Someone asked, but they all shook their heads. The noise was getting louder now, a low, rumbling sound.

"Bloody hell!" Bernie yelled as the source of the noise came around the bend in the road.

Mary's first thought was that it was a tank. It had the shape of something from an old war movie, with huge tracks along the bottom where it was churning up the snow. It was made of metal, with no windows, only a boxy shape with a sort of button on the top. As Mary watched, she realised a figure was poking out of the top, but she couldn't see much of them.

"They've sent the army to get us!" She said, giving the newcomers a wave.

"Is that a tank?" Liz asked.

"Some sort of armoured personnel carrier," the farmer said. "Not a real tank. There's no gun on the top, do you see?"

"Looks like a tank to me," Mary said happily. She would have welcomed an ice-cream van if it had managed up the road to the cottage.

The rumbling sound continued as the vehicle made its way up to the cottage. It juddered up the steep hill without slipping, only nudging the stricken jeep very slightly on its way past. Finally, it arrived in front of the cottage.

For a moment, no one said a thing as it steamed in the snowy air.

"I still think it looks like a tank," Liz muttered.

There was something deeply weird about this thing that should have been in a war zone somewhere being on the front drive of a cottage in Scotland. Mary rubbed her eyes, but when she pulled her hands away, the huge metal vehicle was still there. It couldn't be real, could it?

The tank-thing made a series of robotic noises as whoever was inside turned off the engine.

Now that it was in front of them, Mary could see that there was indeed a figure on top of the tank wearing a headset. It gave them a wave. There was something in the way they stood that seemed familiar.

"Oh my god!" Mary put her hand to her mouth

"Is that… that's not your boyfriend, is it?" Liz asked.

"I think it might be."

Walker pulled off his headset and climbed down from the roof of the tank-thing.

"Bloody hell," Liz whispered. "If you don't marry that man, Mary, I'm going to do it."

"Liz Okoro, you are already married. And pregnant," Bernie tutted.

"He came to save us in a tank!" Liz hissed back. "Dave would understand."

Mary, for her part, was speechless.

"Hello," Walker said as he walked up to the house.

"Hello," the women chorused back.

"I heard you might be in a bit of trouble," Walker said. Now that he was at the house, he looked a little embarrassed. "I was worried. About Liz and the baby. Um. And about the rest of you. I thought you might need some help."

Mary stepped forward and gave his arm a squeeze. "You have no idea how right you are. There's been a murder."

"You're not... that's not just a funny quote, is it? You're serious?"

It took the best part of twenty minutes to explain the situation to Walker. The driver of what it turned out was an armoured personnel carrier was having a cup of tea in the kitchen before he took them down to Aviemore.

"I'm going to stay here with Viola," Walker said. In his defence, he hadn't looked too shocked when they told him that she had been moved into the garage. Mary was finding his professional manner and I'm-in-charge attitude very alluring, not that she would tell him that.

"We can pack all of the women into the APC to go to Aviemore. The farmer too."

"And the stripper."

"The what?"

"And the stripper's dad. It's a long story."

Walker took a deep breath. "Of course there's a stripper. Well, it'll be cramped, but I'm guessing no one will complain as long as we get you all out of here."

Bernie turned up at his elbow as if from nowhere. "I'm staying too."

"Sorry, what?"

"I'm staying here. You need someone who was here all weekend to explain the situation to you. And that's me."

By this point, Walker had the glassy-eyed stare that he seemed to adopt when presented with Bernie Paterson.

"You want to stay here with me? Just the two of us?"

"It's the only option," Bernie said, in a voice that brooked no discussion.

131

"Oh. Right then. Everyone else into the tank. I mean, armoured personnel carrier. Let's get you out of here."

Chapter 18: Liz

Liz had experienced some amazing moments in her life. The birth of her first child was definitely up there. Well, not the birth itself, obviously, which was all noise and pain and pushing, but the sense of becoming a mum, that had been awesome. And her wedding day had been pretty good. A holiday with Dave when they had first started going out to Egypt to see the pyramids had been sensational. But nothing, not one single thing in her life felt as good as driving away from that bloody cottage.

The tank, or rather, the armoured personnel carrier, was not exactly comfortable. The bench seating rattled with every movement from the treads on the icy road. And the noise was like being in a blender. But at least they were moving. The cottage was behind them, and the metropolis of Aviemore was in their near future.

"I hope Walker is all right," Mary said. She had to shout it into Liz's ear twice before she understood what the woman was saying.

"He's a policeman. He's seen his fair share of dead bodies, I'm sure."

"It's not that. I don't mind leaving him with a corpse. It's leaving him with Bernie that I'm worried about."

"I'm sure she'll be on her best behaviour."

"Are you?"

"No. But as long as I get away from the hen-do from hell, I don't care."

After about twenty minutes, Hailey started shouting something down the other end of the tank. Liz couldn't make it out, but she could see that Hailey was pointing at her phone. Soon, the women around her were pulling out their own mobiles.

"Reception's back!" Mary said with a grin, just as Liz checked her phone. Sadly it was far too loud to make any calls, but she managed to send off a quick 'I'm fine' message to Dave. A feeling of relief washed over her. They were heading back to civilisation, and they weren't alone any longer. She put her hand on her bump, sensing a release of tension that she hadn't realised was there.

It took them less than an hour to reach Aviemore in the end, which was extraordinary, when you considered how isolated they had been in the cottage. Not that Liz realised that they had arrived in the town until the vehicle started to slow down. It wasn't like there were any windows to look out of.

They drove to the police station first, as they had agreed at the cottage. When the armoured personnel carrier came to a stop, the farmer popped his head back down into the main chamber.

"Let's get you lot out of here."

Despite her additional weight, Liz was first to leave through the rear door, escaping the stale air and emerging into the light like she had been underground for years, rather than an hour.

Aviemore was quiet, the snow muffling the sound. The main road had been cleared, but everywhere else looked blocked off. The police station was right in front of them, and their transportation was blocking the road.

Liz's first thought when she saw the police station was that it was tiny. The station in Invergryff backed onto a council office block, and the building was a huge grey monstrosity with tiny windows and concrete walls. Here, the police station looked more like the sort of bungalow your granny would retire in. It was a long, low building with a grey roof and square windows. As Liz waited for the others to make their way down from the hatch onto the pavement, she noticed that half a dozen people had come out to see what the hell had just parked outside.

"You can't park that thing here!" A man with a large beard and an equally large stomach shouted.

The driver of the tank-thing grinned. "I'm not staying, just dropping off."

"You're Evan, aren't you? The guy that does the off-roading."

"Aye. These folk were trapped in the snow up in the cottage off the back road. Will Laurel's place. That's him getting the bags. You could say that there's been a bit of a commotion."

That was some understatement, Liz thought. She stepped forward.

"There was a death while we were at the cottage. A woman called Viola Gordon."

"A death?" The bearded man frowned. "You better come inside and make a statement."

"All of us?" Hailey asked.

"Ah, well. We've only got one interview room," the copper said, looking at the group of them in dismay. "And two cells."

"I'm not going into the bloody cells," Hailey said firmly. "Why don't you find a hotel or something where you can put us all up?"

"Actually, that's not a bad idea," the man replied. He turned to a young constable and told her to make the arrangements. The woman scurried off into the building, already on her phone.

In the next few minutes they had all shuffled out of the not-a-tank and the driver drove off, with William Laurel playing co-pilot as they went. Apparently it could be driven by just one person, but the police officers had not seemed very keen at all on that idea.

The officer with the beard introduced himself as Sergeant Graeme Hughson. Although he had initially seemed sceptical, to his credit it didn't take him long before he realised that something serious had occurred. This was probably helped by the fact that Liz had shown him pictures of Viola's dead body on her phone.

"Our friend Sergeant Walker is up there right now," Liz explained, while Hughson scrolled the pictures with an increasingly horrified face.

"Walker? I don't know a Sergeant Walker?"

136

"He's from Invergryff, like us. He's actually…" Liz looked across the room at Mary. "He's sort of dating my friend. He was worried about us, so he came up here."

"All right, it seems like your story checks out. But if this is some kind of wind-up…"

Liz pointed at her belly. "Do you think I'm in any condition to be playing games?"

The Sergeant coughed. "Maybe not. I'm going to get some of my constables to escort you to a nearby hotel. I don't want you talking to anyone while you're there. I especially don't want you talking to one another. We'll get you all rooms on the same floor and interview you in due course. Meanwhile, my Inspector will take a full forensic team up to this cottage."

"Thank you," Liz said, relief washing over her.

As most of the squad cars would be needed to go up to the cottage, Sergeant Hughson arranged for two minibuses to take them up to the hotel. There was a brief discussion when the stripper and his father tried to get permission to go home, but Hughson was having none of it. Liz wondered if he had been a little annoyed by the fact that the stripper was still wearing his sexy policeman costume, including the rubber baton.

No one spoke to each other as they rode the minibuses over to the North end of Aviemore. It was amazing to think it had only been two days ago that they had gotten off the train, excited and anticipating a fun weekend. And now look at them. Mary was on her phone, Nora and Pru were staring out of the window, not talking to each other. They were a miserable bunch. Hailey and Trystesse were on the other minibus with the stripper and his father. Liz wondered if she should try and bolster a sense of community, get them all talking to each other, but she was just too exhausted.

They pulled up outside a hotel that looked a little too much like the setting for a Stephen King film for Liz's liking. It was Victorian at the front, with some dodgy looking flat-roofed extensions on the side and back. The paint was peeling off the sign, and there didn't seem to be many inhabitants.

"It was the only place that still had rooms," a police Constable said, giving her a hand down from the minibus.

"I can see why," Liz said.

"We could try somewhere else if you like," the Constable said.

"No, it's fine. It's a million times better than the bloody cottage anyway."

There was a general milling around while the police officers went to find out their room numbers. While they were waiting, a young man came out of the entrance to the hotel.

"Oh crap," Hailey said quietly. "It's Alfie."

Liz raised her eyebrows. "You don't mean Alfie, as in Viola's fiancé, do you?"

Hailey nodded, her lips pressed together so tightly they had drained of colour.

"Does he know?" Mary asked.

"How would he," Hailey said. "I mean, we've only just informed the police. What the hell do we do?"

The man spotted the women, standing awkwardly a few feet away and gave them a jaunty wave.

"We just get on with it," Liz said, more confidently than she felt. "We're about to ruin the poor guy's life, how we go about it doesn't matter."

"I'll tell him," Hailey said, her voice shaking. "But would you... I mean, I know we haven't exactly been getting on for the last few days, but would you come with me? I don't think I can do it on my own."

Liz and Mary stepped forward as one. "Of course we will," Liz said. "We'll do it together."

Chapter 19: Bernie

Bernie watched while Sergeant Walker examined the body of Viola Gordon.

"You shouldn't have moved her, you know," he said.

She rolled her eyes. "I know. But I had a house full of panicking civilians, so I didn't have much choice. Plus, there was the temperature question."

Walker nodded. "It's certainly cold enough in here. I'm freezing my b... my toes off."

He pointed at Viola's nose. "Is that blood around the nostrils?"

Bernie nodded. "There were spots of blood on the pillowcase."

"You can show me when we go up to the room." Walker sat back on his heels. He had been very careful not to touch the body. Too careful for Bernie's liking: she was hoping to see an examination of Viola that might give her a better idea of who killed the woman. What was the point in having a cop around if he didn't do any further examinations? If nothing else, he could have had a root around in Viola's clothing, but apparently that would have 'disturbed evidence'.

"She was cold when you found her, is that right?"

"Yes," Bernie answered. "That was at six-thirty."

"Had rigor set in?"

She shrugged. "There was some stiffness in the body, but I'm not a doctor. I wouldn't like to say."

"I don't suppose you've worked out who did it yet?" Walker asked.

"Not yet. We've got a spreadsheet, though, with everyone's movements and possible motives."

"Of course you have. And no one heard anything in the night?"

"No. Mary, Liz and I went to bed early, and the others were too drunk to notice anything."

Walker ran a hand across his forehead. "I suppose if Viola had been sleeping deeply, there might not have been much noise when someone was smothering her."

"Especially if she had been drugged."

"Drugged?" Walker raised an eyebrow.

"Come inside and I'll show you the glass."

Despite Bernie's urgings, Walker spent another twenty minutes making sure that he hadn't missed anything in the garage. No wonder the police never solved anything important, Bernie thought, they were so infuriatingly slow! Finally, the police officer followed her inside where they climbed the stairs and entered Viola's room.

If Mary or Liz had been there, they would no doubt have wittered on about the strange atmosphere in the room. The single dirty sock left on the floor or the open bottle of moisturizer on the bedside table would become great tragic symbols. But Bernie had spent all of her working life being around death, and she knew that that was just the human urge to look for meaning where there was none. Yes, it was sad that a woman had died in such a way, but there was no point in getting irrational about it.

Walker, Bernie was glad to see, was of a similar mind. Instead of bemoaning Viola's death, he walked carefully around the room, taking note of each and every item, looking for anything that might be out of place.

"Was the pillow sitting like that when you found her?" Walker asked, gesturing to the pillow that was positioned halfway down the bed.

"Yes. You can see here the depression where her body was on the left-hand side. I didn't touch the pillow and neither did anyone else."

The police officer looked at it closely, still not touching anything. "That's definitely blood spots there. Most likely this was used for the act of suffocation."

"I had worked that out," Bernie reminded him.

"Would you mind standing over in the doorway," Walker said. "So that I can walk around the room unhindered."

Bernie was a bit annoyed at this, but did as the man asked. It was against her nature to accept instructions, but she was finding it fascinating to watch Walker work. She was taking mental notes for her next WWC crime scene.

"That's the glass over there," she said, pointing to the bedside table so that he wouldn't miss it. He walked around and bent down towards the glass.

Walker sniffed it. "The smell is familiar."

"Cyanide?" Bernie said, squeezing in next to him. "Isn't that what they say in Agatha Christie? Almonds, wasn't it? Very good for the micronutrients. I often have a handful for a snack. Or strychnine. Although I don't know what kind of nut that smells like."

"I don't think there are any nuts involved. I think it is soluble aspirin."

"What?"

"Yeah, she probably had a sore head in the night and made herself one. Nothing to do with her murder."

"Oh. That is disappointing." Bernie would not have admitted it to anyone, but she was feeling rather deflated. There was nothing she liked better than outsmarting the constabulary, but so far there was nothing to show Walker that would impress him.

"I want to say thank you," the Sergeant said as they left Viola's room.

"For what?" Bernie asked.

"For keeping everyone calm. Mary told me how you took

charge. There could have been a real panic here otherwise."

"Well, that bunch of softies needed someone to take the reins," Bernie said, allowing herself a smile.

"I'm sure they did. Now, you said something about a spreadsheet?"

"That's right. We've done a detailed timeline of Friday night, where everyone was at various points in the evening. Of course, someone has to be lying, but it might help. And then there's everything we found during the searches."

"The searches?"

"Yes. We conducted searches of everyone's belongings last night."

Walker groaned. "Please tell me you had their consent."

"They didn't not consent, if you see what I mean. Seeing as they didn't know about it."

"Bernie, you can't just do that –"

"Lecture me when you're sharing a house with a killer, won't you?"

Walker's shoulders slumped. "Fine. Did your gross invasion of privacy discover anything?"

"Oh plenty, but that's the trouble. Everyone has their secrets, but how many of them might lead to murder?"

"Well, one, clearly," Walker said. Bernie felt that he wasn't quite getting into the spirit of it.

"I do have something else for you," Bernie said, reaching into her pocket. "But you have to agree that you'll let me have a look at it too when you get the password.

A frown line appeared between Walker's eyebrows. "Are you trying to blackmail me?"

She sighed. Why was everyone so dramatic? "Not at all. I just thought you might want to help the person that discovered vital evidence thrown away into the snow." She passed over the plastic bag with the phone in it.

"Is this Viola's?" Walker asked, taking it and peering at the phone through the plastic.

"No. It's Hailey's. Which is rather suggestive, don't you think?"

"And you saw her throw it outside?"

"Not quite. Someone got up last night when it was dark and left it buried in the snow, but I couldn't say for sure it was Hailey, just that it was one of the hen party. Hailey had mentioned that she thought someone had taken her phone earlier that day. Of course, she could well be lying."

"Password protected," Walker said as he tapped the home button. "I'm guessing you haven't managed to get a look at the messages."

"No. I would have waited for the police anyway."

"Liar," Walker laughed. "I'll get this over to the technical team when I get to Aviemore."

"And you'll tell me what's on it?"

"We'll see," Walker said in a way that Bernie found very irritating. "Can I see that spreadsheet now?"

Feeling like she was giving the man a whole lot for not a lot of co-operation, Bernie passed her laptop over to the police officer.

"Lucky you brought this with you," he said while he scrolled through the spreadsheet.

"We were doing work on the train, so the whole trip is tax deductible," Bernie explained.

"Are you sure that... No, never mind, let's focus on the task at hand." He peered at the document. "Hang on, you've got listings here for Mary and Liz's rooms."

It wasn't often that Bernie blushed, but she could feel her cheeks flush with heat.

"Ah, I meant to take those out."

"Why on earth would you... did you search their rooms too?"

"Only in the interest of thoroughness."

"And I'm guessing you didn't mention it to either of them."

Bernie looked up at the ceiling. "They would only have complained."

146

"You're a piece of work, Bernie Paterson," Walker said, his eyes still on the spreadsheet.

"Thank you," Bernie replied.

Chapter 20: Walker

The snow had melted sufficiently to allow the ambulance to make it up the drive to the cottage by eleven in the morning, which was lucky as Walker was on the verge of committing murder himself. Bernie had never left his side while he investigated the crime scene, and he had discovered that he could only tolerate her company in very small doses. When the ambulance turned up, he told Bernie to wait inside the cottage while he went to meet the paramedics. Walker had warned them about the roads, but they still looked ashen-faced by the time they made it up the drive. He made them a cup of tea each – it wasn't like there was any particular hurry where Viola Gordon was concerned – then showed them into the garage.

"Nothing much we can do until the forensics team okay us to move the body," the older paramedic explained.

"They should be here any minute," Walker said, glancing out at the snow. The trees were already dripping with snowmelt. By evening it would be as if the storm had never touched the place. You could almost imagine that nothing untoward had happened.

The noise of sirens came from the road. Four police cars, two unmarked and two with their lights on, drove up to the house.

Not so easy to imagine nothing had happened now, Walker thought as he walked out to meet the dozen people that had just arrived.

The Senior Investigating Officer was a man Walker hadn't met before named Inspector Adam MacLeish. Technically it should have been a CID case, but as MacLeish explained:

"The plainclothes lads are all in Inverness. They'll be down when the road opens. Whenever that might be."

MacLeish had thick black bushy eyebrows that gave every facial expression an added emphasis. Walker was trying his best not to stare at them.

"We've put the hen party up in the hotel, and my Sergeant will be interviewing them as we speak. Can you explain to me again your connection with the deceased?"

"I never met her," Walker said. "My... girlfriend is Mary Plunkett, one of the women on the hen-do. Her friend Liz is pregnant, so when we hadn't heard from them for a while, we started getting worried. I saw that the weather was bad and I thought they might be in trouble. Of course, I didn't imagine it would be anything like this."

"And do you usually turn up in a tank when you haven't heard from your girlfriend for a few hours?"

Walker felt the blush creep up his cheeks. "No, sir. I just... had a bad feeling about them. And the trip was all paid for by me, not on police expenses."

"I would bloody hope so!"

This didn't seem to be going too well. The thing was, Walker could hardly blame the Inspector for being sceptical. The whole scenario was strange enough, without the dead body. With the body in the garage, it was all looking very suspicious, and Walker didn't blame the Inspector for not trusting him. And the whole armoured personnel carrier thing hadn't done him any favours.

The cottage and the garage were crawling with the forensic technicians in their plastic suits. Hopefully, they would find some evidence of who had murdered Viola. Otherwise it was a case of too many suspects to go around.

"You know all the women involved, do you?" MacLeish asked.

Walker shook his head. "Only Mary and the other members of the WWC."

"The what?"

He swallowed. "The, um... the Wronged Women's Co-operative. They're a private investigation agency based in Invergryff. They've actually been quite helpful in our cases in the past."

MacLeish's eyebrows waggled their way upwards. "You mean to say I've had a bunch of true crime aficionados bumbling around my crime scene?"

"Well, they're not quite that bad, sir. They're a professional outfit. And Bernie Paterson, the boss, is a qualified nurse, so she knew what she was doing."

"She's the one that moved the body, I take it?"

"Yes sir."

The eyebrows were not happy, and it showed. "I'll put her at the top of our interview list. And you can tell your girlfriend that we don't hold with people messing about in police investigations in the Highlands, all right?"

"Yes sir."

Mollified by Walker's contrite expression, the eyebrows climbed back down his forehead. Just as Bernie stepped out of the cottage.

"Are you here to give me a lift back to town?" she asked MacLeish before Walker could even introduce them. "I need to speak to my fellow investigators."

"Actually, I'm here to examine the crime scene. You wouldn't be Bernie Paterson, by any chance?"

Bernie grinned. "Good to know that my reputation precedes me. Do you want to interview me before or after you drop me off at the hotel?"

MacLeish was starting to put on the slightly bemused expression that people often wore when talking to Bernie.

"I do have rather a lot to be going on with here. Seeing as I am the Senior Investigating Officer, you see."

"I'm sure good delegation is the hallmark of every competent Inspector," Bernie said. "I believe your forensic team have finished in the living room, so perhaps we could conduct the interview in there. The sofa is quite sturdy and not too hard on the lumbar muscles. The stripper said it was comfortable to sleep on last night."

"The stripper?"

"It's all in my notes, sir," Walker murmured.

The eyebrows lowered in resignation. "Give me half an hour to speak to my officers, then I will interview you in the living room. All right?"

"Perfect," Bernie beamed. "Any chance of a cup of tea first? Your men in plastic suits have taken over the kitchen and I'm absolutely gasping."

Walker didn't have to see the Inspector's face to know it was time to get Bernie out of there. He took her firmly by the arm and steered her into the living room.

"Do you ever think about toning it down a little with new people," he said to the woman as she commandeered the corner position on the sofa.

"You need to keep the enemy on their toes," Bernie said, plumping a cushion and placing it behind her back. "I'm David and the Inspector over there is Goliath. I have to use everything I can to keep my advantage."

"We're not on opposing sides, Bernie," Walker said, trying to keep a lid on his mounting irritation. "We all want to find out who murdered your friend."

"That's not strictly true, though, is it? Because as far as your Inspector is concerned, Mary, Liz and I are suspects just as much as the rest of them. It's not just Viola's killer that we're trying to find out this time. We're also trying to save the reputation of the Wronged Women's Co-operative. And that's much more important."

Walker let his eyes drift to the ceiling while he counted to ten.

"I might go and see if I can help in the garage," Walker said, edging towards the door.

"Oh, I shouldn't think they'll want your help. A copper from the Lowlands, stomping all over their crime scene, turning up in a tank of all things. I imagine they think you're quite the fool."

"I'll just go and find out then, won't I," Walker snarled, closing the door behind him. He tried to pretend that he couldn't hear Bernie cackling with laughter as he left.

Chapter 21: Mary

It was rather wonderful to have a room of her own, Mary realised. Even if there was a police Constable standing outside to make sure she didn't go AWOL. She had no intentions of anything of the sort, of course. Since Walker had arrived, like Sir Lancelot on his steed, only rather more up-to-date and metallic, Mary had known that everything would be okay. They would find Viola's killer and she would be back to the kids in no time.

The police officers had allowed her to put in a video call to Matt, and just seeing their wee faces had washed away much of the horror of the last couple of days. It hadn't even mattered that Johnny had shown her how his wobbly tooth could turn right the way around, or that Vicky and Peter had barely looked up from their tablets. A shouted 'love you mum' was all she had needed.

She had even allowed herself a little cry afterwards. The thing was, it was one thing to be investigating murders for a living, but quite another for it to happen right next to you. Poor Viola, Mary hadn't even known her that well, but no one deserved their life to end like that.

And telling her fiancé about Viola's death had been a million kinds of awful. At first, Alfie had thought it was a joke, then he had broken down in tears. His brother, Howie, a big guy built like a rugby player, had taken him inside to calm down. Mary guessed they would be under house arrest too. The

154

partner was always the first person the police suspected, but Mary couldn't see how anyone from outside the house could have been involved. Still, they would need to check out his background when they got the chance.

Mary turned on her laptop. She didn't have the spreadsheet from Bernie yet, but the woman had promised she would send it once she had wifi access. Poor Bernie, still stuck at that cottage. And poor Walker, stuck with Bernie. Still, Mary had made a start on her collection of notes about the case.

One of the areas where she realised she needed to do some more work was her section of information about the victim. It should have been easy, really. They had all known Viola for several months, had spent nights out with her, and had several afternoon teas together. But it turned out they hadn't learned much about her background.

Born in Invergryff, she had spent her time between her mother's council house in one of the less affluent suburbs of the town, and her dad's place in London. It must have been a strange childhood, Mary thought, swapping between the two places. Both Pru and Nora had mentioned that Viola was obsessed with money, and that was understandable for someone growing up in poverty.

Mary tried to think if Viola had ever shown that part of her character in front of her. There were the expensive bags and shoes, of course, although Mary hadn't taken much notice of them. She had always preferred quirky things over designer labels.

When she still lived with Matt, Mary had been able to buy

whatever she liked. Living in the oil rich city of Aberdeen she had spent time with other similarly affluent housewives and never had to think about what she was spending. Of course, she hadn't realised that it was all a sham, Matt's having gambled away all the money long before she noticed it was gone. Was it the same for Viola? Was she living on credit, giving a false impression of being able to afford all the posh clothes that she wore? It was possible. Mary made a note to ask Liz about it, as she was the financial expert.

There had been one time, Mary remembered, when Viola had said something about money. They had gone out to a restaurant in Glasgow for Bernie's birthday. When it came time to order a bottle of wine, Mary had opted for her usual 'second cheapest bottle on the menu'. Viola had insisted on Champagne. There had been a moment of awkwardness before she offered to pay for it herself, but that was it. Flashy with money might not be a particularly pleasant personality trait, but it was hardly a motive for murder.

Time for some deep online stalking. Investigating was so much easier when you had internet access. The police officers had asked them not to talk to each other, but they hadn't said anything about staying off social media. Mary opened up her usual apps and had a look at Viola's profiles.

Viola was definitely a fan of having an online presence. She was on all the same apps as Mary, and a couple of others as well. Mary settled in to flick through the photographs. There were loads of Viola and her fiancé, their smiling faces giving Mary a twinge of pain as she looked at them. There were expensive holidays abroad, photos of them in swanky cocktail bars, the usual stuff that might come under the category of 'influencer'. When Mary clicked through to Alfie's page that seemed to be his primary profession. Didn't he work for his family's hotel chain? Mary scrolled past post after post of fancy cars and nights out with the lads. There didn't seem to be any pictures of his work, but then maybe he just didn't bother to take any.

Alfie and Viola had been together for not much more than a year, and Mary's inner gossip was excited to find out that he hadn't deleted the pictures of his previous girlfriend. She had been very beautiful, with long black hair and a curvy body that she showed off in figure-hugging outfits. Viola, with her more athletic figure and designer trouser suits, came off as almost demure in comparison. A little further digging and Mary learned that the ex-girlfriend's name was Uma Singh. Mary added her name to the spreadsheet.

Unfortunately, it wasn't so easy to find any of Viola's exes. All of her photos taken earlier than a couple of years ago had been deleted. Mary made a note to ask Nora and Pru if there had been anyone serious before Alfie. Not that they would be a suspect, most likely, but it helped to round out the picture of Viola in her mind.

Mary's phone buzzed and she answered it immediately when she saw Walker's name.

"I've just left the cottage," he explained. "I'm in the ambulance right now."

"Are you… is Viola there with you?" Mary shivered at the idea.

157

"Yes. We'll be stopping at the hospital, then I'm coming over to the hotel. Are you getting on okay?"

"Fine. They've split us all up into separate rooms, but to be honest I'm grateful for the peace."

"Bernie's on her way too. She's blagged a lift with the Inspector, but I don't think he's very happy about it. Listen, this isn't going to be like in Invergryff. MacLeish doesn't want any involvement from the WWC, and there's nothing I can do about that. I'm just an intruder in his case, as far as he's concerned."

"I'm sure that's not true."

Walker chuckled. "You ever seen a nature show where gorillas defend their territory by ripping their enemies' arms off? The police force is like that, only more territorial. I'll have to fade into the background now that I've got you out of that cottage."

"Did I say thank you for that, by the way?" Mary asked.

"About a hundred times. And so did Liz and the rest of the hens. The stripper even gave me a hug, which is something I'm not going to forget for a while."

"He did have impressive abs," Mary said. "Will I see you soon?"

"This afternoon, hopefully. I've got to give my statement, and you'll have to do yours, so it will be after that."

"All right," she said, trying not to sound too needy. Mind you, when you had been trapped in a snowstorm, cut off from

158

civilisation and in the company of a corpse, maybe you were allowed to be a little more vulnerable than usual.

Walker said goodbye and Mary went back to scrolling through social media posts with Viola in them. She came across Nora's photos and flicked through them quickly. Nora Woods didn't have much of a social media presence, preferring to keep most things private. This was frustrating, until Mary came across her business page, 'Luxury by Eleanora'. Here there were plenty of photos, mainly before and after shots of clients. It didn't take long for Mary to find several shots of Viola looking happy with new highlights or a manicure.

Woman gets manicure. It wasn't exactly the startling insight that Mary was looking for. She was about to close down the page when she saw something that made her do a double-take. Six months ago one of the clients for Nora's hair before and after shots was Trystesse MacKinnon. Her face was in profile to show off the hair, but Mary was sure it was her. Had Nora mentioned that she knew Trystesse before the hen-do? Mary was sure she hadn't.

It might not mean anything, and yet... Bernie had always said to make a note of anything weird, so Mary typed it into the spreadsheet. Perhaps Trystesse and Nora had planned the murder together? It seemed extraordinary, but someone had to have killed Viola, so why not them?

Mary got up and paced around the room. She was starting to feel the same claustrophobia in the hotel that she had felt in the cottage. If only she could speak to Liz or Bernie and plan things out together. She was sure they would have better ideas about who might be the murderer than she did. Sighing, she reached for the kettle to make a sad cup of tea with UHT milk. She hated the taste, but it would give her something to do.

Mary spotted something next to the kettle and picked it up. It was a packet of complimentary shortbread biscuits. With chocolate chips. Mind you, she considered, tearing into the foil, things could be worse.

Chapter 22: Liz

The first thing Liz did when she got to her hotel room was lay down on the bed, closed her eyes and settled in for a good long nap.

However, sleep did not come, no matter how tightly she screwed her eyes shut. Eventually, feeling more fed up than ever, she did the ungainly roll that meant she could sit up from her bed without damaging her back muscles. She checked her phone, but there were no new messages since she had called Dave when they arrived at the hotel. It had choked her up a little how relieved he had sounded to hear from her. Ridiculous, really, when it had only been a couple of days. But Dave was one of those men that turned into a worrier as soon as the baby bump appeared. Of course, this time his worry had turned out to be justified, but as she had told him on the phone, it hadn't been *her* that had been murdered.

Poor Viola. Liz couldn't help but feel that if they had chosen to have the hen-do in a hotel like this one rather than the cottage in the woods, she might still be alive.

There was a knock at the door and Liz got up to answer it, glad that she hadn't fallen asleep after all.

A female police officer with bobbed ginger hair and freckles across her nose stood at the door.

"Is it all right to come in?" She asked.

"Of course," Liz said. There was a single chair at the dressing table, so Liz let the other woman have that while she sat on the edge of the bed.

"I'm Ruby Callaghan and I'm here to take your statement. Before we start, would you like a glass of water?" The woman glanced nervously at Liz's bump.

"I'm fine thank you," Liz said.

"All right. If I can start by taking some personal details. What is it you do for a living?"

This should be interesting, Liz thought. "I'm a private investigator. My friend, Bernie Paterson, set up an agency and I'm her partner."

Callaghan looked shocked, then looked down at her tablet for a moment. "You're a private investigator. But you just happened to be on a hen do where there was a murder, right?"

"That's correct."

The woman stared at her for a second, then went back to her script. "How did you know the deceased?"

"We met through the school. I think it was Bernie that got to know her first. No, that's not right, I met her before that. She was good at doing nails, not those super long ones that the youngsters like, but proper manicures, you know? She offered to do mine, so I went round to her place."

"Where was this?"

162

"A flat overlooking the Abbey. Nice place, very silver and glittery if you know what I mean."

"And she asked you to come on her hen-do?"

"Yes. Me, Bernie and Mary. We all work together at the agency, and we had all met Viola a few times. We were sort of surprised to be asked, but then, by the sound of it so was everyone else."

"What do you mean?"

Liz sighed, trying to think how to explain. "Well, it felt like we were all sort of second-tier friends. Apart from Hailey, none of us spent that much time with Viola, but we were the ones invited to the hen-do. I felt a bit sorry for her, to be honest. Like, if we were her closest friends then she didn't have many at all."

Callaghan nodded. "Did you know her fiancé?"

"Never met him until this morning, poor lad."

"And you can't think of anyone that might have wanted to harm Viola?"

"That's what's so weird about the whole thing," Liz explained. "Because none of us knew her that well, no one had a reason to want her dead. We were doing our own investigations from the moment we knew it was murder, but we didn't come up with much. Bernie has a spreadsheet you should have a look at."

The young woman sniffed. "I'll be sure to do that," she said, in

163

a tone that said she couldn't care less about it. Liz wasn't bothered. She was used to being written off by the constabulary, and it only made it more fun when the WWC got to the finish before they did.

"On the Friday night, did you notice anything unusual about Viola?"

"No. She wasn't scared or worried, as far as I could tell."

"She didn't mention any worries about the wedding?"

"The wedding?" Liz frowned. "Why would she be worried about the wedding?"

Callaghan gave her a tight little smile. "Well, brides often feel nervous, don't they?"

"If anything she was excited," Liz explained. "I think Viola quite liked a bit of attention, and the big wedding suited her."

"What about Alfie? Do you think he was nervous?"

"As I said, I only met him today."

"Right." The woman scrolled down her list of questions. "And if we just get back to Friday night for a second, no one saw anyone enter the house. Or heard anything like that."

Liz shook her head. "No. To be honest, I can't see how someone would have got in without one of us hearing something."

"Weren't you all asleep when Viola was killed?"

"Yes. But as Bernie said, there was no water on the floor."

Callaghan glanced up at her. "Why would that matter?"

"There was snow everywhere outside. If anyone had come in, they would have left wet footprints at the very least. We didn't see any sign of anything like that."

The Constable dropped her eyes back to her tablet. "We'll see what the forensics say," she said. Liz took a deep breath but resisted the urge to argue back. There were several more questions, but Liz made sure to answer with the bare facts, not give her opinion. If the woman wasn't willing to hear her out, then there was no reason to give her any more information than necessary.

Eventually, Callaghan left the room to conduct another interview. Liz sat on the bed for a few moments, thinking back over the conversation. She might have been wrong, but Callaghan had given her the distinct impression that the police were considering Alfie to be the prime suspect. Now, why would that be? Bernie had been convinced that someone on the hen-do had killed Viola, but was there the possibility that Bernie Paterson had got it wrong?

Chapter 23: Bernie

Bernie was not very happy at being sent to a bedroom in the hotel where the rest of the civilians were staying. She had strongly suggested to Inspector MacLeish that it would be better for his investigation if she were allowed into the incident room with the police officers.

For some reason, MacLeish had vetoed the idea. Yet another example of the petty bureaucracy of the police force getting in its own way. Bernie noticed that he had been happy enough to receive a copy of her spreadsheet, however, so he had no problem profiting from the WWC's results without giving them any credit.

She opened the curtains and looked out at the grey Cairngorms sky. The mountains towered over her like ancient gods, reminding the mortals of their puny size. Bernie gave them the finger. People paid good money for this sort of view, but it was murders she was interested in, not silly old hills. And right now she needed to be catching a murderer, not stuck in a room that was basically a police cell, just with a bit more upholstery.

She picked up her phone and called Liz.

"We're not meant to speak to each other," her friend said when she answered the call.

"Balls to that," Bernie replied. "If they were that bothered they'd have taken our phones away. Now tell me what's been happening."

Liz told Bernie all about the trip to Aviemore in the not-a-tank, then the horrible moment where they'd had to break the news to Alfie about the death of his fiancé.

"I think the police were annoyed we hadn't waited for them to do it," Liz said, "but it felt like it should come from someone who knew Viola."

"Quite right," Bernie said. "If we waited around for the police to do everything, you and I would be out of a job."

"There is something a bit funny about all that though," Liz added. "I just had an interview with one of the Constables, and she seemed to be hinting that they considered Alfie a suspect."

"But he wasn't even there?"

"I know. I don't suppose there's any way that someone could have snuck into the cottage from outside on Friday night?"

"Not possible," Bernie replied. She had checked over the cottage herself and there was no sign of any intruder.

"Right."

Bernie looked outside at the hills, lost in thought. "It would be interesting to know exactly why they're considering Alfie as a suspect, however. Maybe he's had a run-in with the police before. Did he tell you why he was in Aviemore?"

"No. That's a good point. Why would he turn up to where Viola was having her hen-do?"

"We need to ask him," Bernie said.

167

"Maybe Mary should do it. She's the best person to deal with someone when they've just had bad news. People always like Mary."

"Or I could do it," Bernie said. "Shake him up a bit and see what falls out."

"I'll call Mary," Liz said and hung up the phone.

Bernie went over to the window. Yep, the mountains were still there, still mountaining. Damn, she was bored.

There was a peephole in the door to her room and she went over to have a look. She couldn't see any sign of a police guard in the corridor. Maybe she could risk it.

As slowly as she could, Bernie eased the door open. It was a fire door, so this was no mean feat. She slipped out and closed it as quietly as possible.

"Can I help you, Mrs Paterson?" A chippy voice called. Just along the corridor, between Bernie and the door to the stairs a female police Constable was sitting on a fold-out seat.

"I thought someone knocked," Bernie said, giving the woman her best glare.

"No one knocked," the woman replied. She had a copy of a newspaper sitting on her knee. "We'd like you to stay in your room please."

Bernie went back inside and shut the door. She opened up her laptop and got to work on the spreadsheet. She could at least do her paperwork while she worked out how the hell she was

168

going to escape from the room.

Chapter 24: Walker

The Aviemore police department had set up an incident room in the hotel where they had placed the hens. Sergeant Graeme Hughson had explained to Walker that there simply wouldn't have been room to set up anything similar in the police station. Besides, it was handy to be on site when there were so many witnesses and so many suspects.

Each member of the hen party had to be considered a subject, and as such their names had been written on a whiteboard in the incident room, which was an abandoned ballroom in the West wing of the hotel. It was a bit of a jolt to see Mary's name up there, along with Bernie and Liz's, but he understood why. It was highly likely that the killer of Viola Gordon was one of the women that had been in the cottage that night. At the moment, not one of them could be eliminated. Hopefully, when the physical evidence was processed, it would give them some indication of who the killer might be, but for the moment they could only rely on the interviews.

The farmer, the stripper and his dad had been interviewed already and released. That had been an interesting conversation. Inspector MacLeish's eyebrows had had a good wander about his face when he'd been confronted with Officer Pantsov. Still, at least it ruled out a few bodies. Often in a murder case, the first few hours were spent finding suspects. The problem in this case was that they already had too many. Seven members of the hen-do meant seven likely suspects, and if Walker was happy to discount the three members of the

WWC, the local police officers weren't likely to do anything of the sort.

"We've conducted the initial interviews with all seven members of the hen-do," MacLeish explained to the rest of the incident room. Walker had snuck in at the back, hoping that if he was quiet then no one would tell him to leave.

"At the moment, the story for each of them matches up. No one saw Viola after she went to bed just before two until they discovered the body the following morning. No one heard anything in the night to suggest foul play. The post mortem won't be until this afternoon, but the pathologist had a quick look at the body for me. At the moment the most likely explanation is death by asphyxiation. We are working on the theory that she was smothered, due to spots of blood on a pillow where the body was found. All of this is just theoretical until the post mortem, but it gives us some indication of what we're looking for."

"Wouldn't she have fought back?" a female Constable asked. "We could be looking for a suspect with scratch marks."

MacLeish shook his head. "She had had a lot to drink. The pathologist reckons she could have been in a sleep so deep that she never woke up at all. Which explains why no one heard anything."

"What about the boyfriend?" Someone asked.

"We're just about to interview him. He's got a bit of a reputation. Investigated for fraud a few years ago. Graeme is going through the old case notes. Nothing violent on his

171

record, however. Plus, there are the roads to factor in. Walker, you were the first one up there, what's the likelihood someone else was there before you."

"Pretty unlikely," Walker said. "Not by road anyway."

"Still, we want to speak to this Alfie character. And we haven't found Viola's phone yet, so we'll need to organise a search of all the women's suitcases before we let them go. Hughson, Beckett, I'll leave that to you."

MacLeish handed out a few more tasks and then the briefing was over. He walked over to where Walker was sitting. "My two Sergeants are busy. Fancy sitting in on the interview with Alfie Callford?"

Walker thought about it for a moment. "Sure, but I wonder if I could bring a friend."

MacLeish's eyes narrowed. "You do like to push your luck, don't you?"

"Always," Walker replied with his most charming smile.

Five minutes later he was knocking on Mary's door.

She opened it rubbing her eyes with her hair in some sort of haystack situation.

"I wasn't sleeping," she said before he could say anything.

Walker leaned forward and brushed his lips against her forehead. "I don't think anyone could blame you for being tired. I was wondering if you wanted to come downstairs."

172

"I'm allowed out?"

"I've cleared it with the guards," he said, relieved to see that she had grabbed a brush and was trying to get her hair to lie flat. "I thought you might like to sit in on an interview with me. It's not going to be a very happy one."

"Who is it?"

"The fiancé. Alfie."

Mary bit her lower lip. "I see. I only met him this morning."

"He's said he's happy to answer questions, but there's a good chance he might be in shock. The Inspector has decided an informal interview in the hotel might be the best way to go, and I thought having one of Viola's friends there might help."

"All right," Mary said.

Walker could tell she was reluctant. "I can get someone else if —"

"No, I'll do it. Bernie would never forgive me if I didn't."

After she had brushed her hair and pulled on some clean clothes, Walker took Mary to a conference room at the back of the hotel. He wasn't sure what the room had been originally, but it had been kitted out in flat-pack furniture and grey wallpaper to meet the standards of business blandness everywhere.

Sitting in the room already were Alfie and his brother Howie. Walker, having never met either man, could tell them apart as

173

Alfie looked like he had been hit by a truck, whereas Howie looked more bored than upset.

Inspector MacLeish was already sitting opposite them at the large conference table. He got up to greet Mary and lead her to a seat strategically positioned in between the police officers and the civilians.

"This is Sergeant Walker. As I've said already, I'm Inspector MacLeish from Police Scotland. We've asked Mary Plunkett to sit in with us today. She was at the cottage and she might be able to help with some of your questions."

Alfie gave Mary a quick nod of recognition, then went back to staring at the table.

"We wanted to ask a few questions about your fiancée. This is just an informal interview. As you can imagine, this isn't our usual way of doing things, but we're on the back foot. We are hoping that the Major Crimes unit will be able to get here later today, or tomorrow morning."

"Why are we here if we're only going to have to go through all this again with the proper cops," the brother said, glaring at the police officers. "My brother's having an absolute nightmare day. Can't you leave him alone?"

The Inspector wasn't fazed by the man's bluster. "We have an investigation to conduct. I'm sure your brother understands. The sooner we get our answers, the sooner we can find out what happened to Viola."

"And you don't think it could just have been an accident?"

Howie suggested. "I mean, if they were all drunk, you hear things about people dying suddenly like that."

"I'm afraid we have good reason to suspect foul play," the Inspector said. "That's why we would like to be sure we get all the details as quickly as we can."

"All right," Alfie said. "Ask your questions."

"Can you tell us how and when you first met your fiancée?"

"We met at a party at my parent's hotel. They sometimes host charity evenings. I think it was a kids' cancer charity. You pay for a table, and Viola was there with some friends."

"When was this?"

"Eighteen months ago. We hit it off, and that was it. She was the first... well, before her it had never been serious."

"And the wedding was planned for the summer?"

Alfie sniffed. "Yes. In June. She wanted the hen-do to be in the Easter holidays because it was easier to get time off. She worked in a school, you see."

"And you work for your parent's business, is that right?"

"Yes. I'm the media manager. I'm a content creator too."

"Three hundred thousand followers on the clock app," Howie said, as if that meant something. Maybe it did if you were interested in influencer types. Walker didn't understand any of that stuff. It made him feel old.

175

MacLeish looked down at his notes. "And as far as you know, there was nothing worrying Viola? Nothing about the wedding?"

"Why would there be?" Alfie asked, his bottom lip jutting out.

"Brides can be nervous sometimes, can't they?"

Alfie's shoulder started to tremble. "You think she wasn't going to go through with it? No way, all she'd talked about for the last few months was the wedding. I've had enough of this."

He stood up, ready to leave, but Mary stood up too, getting between him and the door.

"I know how much Viola was looking forward to the wedding," she said gently. "It was all she could talk about at the hen-do. I know she wanted to be your wife. And she would want you to help these police officers find out exactly what happened to her."

Mary's soft voice unlocked a little of the tension in Alfie's shoulders and he sat back down.

"Just get on with it," he said to MacLeish, rubbing his sleeve over his eyes.

"Why did you come up to Aviemore this weekend?" the Inspector asked.

"It was Howie's idea. He said it would be a good laugh. After all, it's not like Aviemore is a clubbing hotspot. He said Viola would be bored stiff up here, and he was right. I thought I'd show up with some bottles of champagne, film her reaction, all that stuff. I thought it would be a laugh," he repeated forlornly.

Walker looked to the brother to see if he would agree with this, but the man was downing a glass of water. "This place is a dump," Howie said, refilling his glass from a jug. "Not even bottled water. We booked rooms in the new hotel up the road. They've got two swimming pools."

"Was it your idea to come up here?" MacLeish prompted.

"I guess so. Yeah, I think I suggested it. We didn't have anything else planned, so why not?"

Howie was definitely being cagey, but Walker knew MacLeish couldn't push him too far, not in this informal interview scenario.

"We've been looking into Viola's finances," MacLeish said, changing the subject. "She seems to have a healthy bank account for a school secretary."

Alfie managed a smile. "Nah, that was just, like, her day job. She was a proper entrepreneur. I was helping her grow her social media and stuff."

"And that's where the money came from? Social media?"

"A bit of advertising, that sort of thing."

MacLeish clasped his hands together. "Still, that's a lot of money without a clear sense of where it came from."

"There's nothing dodgy about it. It's all legit." For the first time Alfie looked shifty, his legs jiggling under the table.

"We'll check it out further," MacLeish said firmly. "But as far as you know, there's no reason that the women at the cottage wanted your fiancé dead?"

"No," Alfie said, the tears welling up in his eyes again. "They were supposed to be her friends."

Chapter 25: Mary

The interview with Alfie took them until after lunch, so it wasn't until after two o'clock that the members of the hen-do were called down to get something to eat. Mary was relieved as the shortbread was long gone and she had been seriously considering munching on the tiny packets of sugar. They were still being kept in a sort of weird quarantine as the hotel had arranged a lunch for them in the conference room she had been in earlier when they had interviewed Alfie.

The interview had been upsetting, and Mary felt like she hadn't been much help to the police. Alfie's grief at Viola's death had seemed genuine to her, and she couldn't see any reason why he would have been involved in the murder. The police seemed to still have him in their sights, but Mary wasn't so sure.

Viola's fiancé was nowhere to be seen at the lunch buffet, but all the members of the hen-do were there, including Bernie who had recently returned from the cottage.

"How did it go with Walker at the crime scene?" Mary asked when she managed to squeeze her way past the buffet queue and corner her friend.

"I don't know how the police get anything done. He didn't examine any of the evidence."

"Well, he'll be waiting for forensics." Mary found herself defending her boyfriend.

"Huh, sounds like an excuse to me. He didn't find out anything that we didn't already know."

Mary made a mental note to give Walker a hug when she next saw him. Bernie sounded like she was in a particularly belligerent mood today.

"I've just come out of the interview with Alfie Callford," Mary told her in a low voice.

This cheered her friend up. "You lucky so and so. How did you manage that?"

"Walker asked me. And I didn't feel particularly lucky. Poor Alfie, he was devastated."

"He could be faking it," Bernie said.

Mary shrugged. It was possible, but it hadn't felt like it when she had been in the room with him. "The police seem to think he might be. They kept asking him about his relationship with Viola. I think they've got him down as prime suspect."

Bernie picked up a piece of cucumber and crunched it. "I still don't see how anyone from outside could have committed the murder, but we'd best not rule him out. He could have been working with one of the hens."

"Which one?"

The nurse thought for a moment. "It could be Hailey. If she had messages from Alfie on her phone, then that would be a reason for her to conveniently lose it."

180

"I'll ask Walker if they've had a chance to look at her phone yet," Mary said.

"Good. I'd love to know what's on it. There she is over in the corner with Trystesse. I'm going to have a little chat with them."

Bernie wandered off, leaving Mary standing awkwardly by herself. She grabbed some tortilla chips and dips so that she had something to do with her hands.

Liz came in and started loading up her plate. "I fell asleep there for an hour," she said when Mary walked over to her. "I'm turning into an old woman."

"You're pregnant," Mary reminded her. "When I was pregnant with Lauren I used to hand the kids a big bag of popcorn, get them to put a film on the telly and have a two hour sleep while they played 'home cinema'. You need your rest."

"Well, you can explain to Bernie that I haven't done any work on the case. She asked me to look into those pregnancy tablets we found, but I haven't got a clue who they belong to."

Mary spotted some brie and cranberry vol au vents and she had a flash of an idea. She picked up the tray and showed them to Liz.

"You don't have to play waitress," Liz said. "People are just helping themselves."

"I know," Mary whispered. "But look at this. Soft cheese!"

"Sorry, what?"

"It's brie. Soft cheese. The sort that you're not allowed in pregnancy."

Mary waggled her eyebrows and saw realization dawn on Liz's face.

"You're going to see if anyone refuses, and that will somehow prove that they're pregnant, will it?"

"It's not the worst idea ever."

"It's not the best," Liz replied. "What if they just don't like brie?"

"At least we'll have narrowed it down," Mary said firmly. She didn't like how Liz was responding to her idea, which she was quite convinced was a genius one.

Holding the tray, she walked over to Pru and Nora. They seemed more subdued than they had been in the cottage and Mary wondered if the two day hangover had kicked in.

"Would you like a brie and cranberry vol au vent?"

"God no, I couldn't eat anything," Pru said.

"Why not?" Mary asked.

"I have the hangover from hell, thanks for asking. Unless you want me to puke all over your wellies, you can do one."

"What about you?" Mary asked, waving the tray under Nora's nose.

"I don't do refined carbs," Nora said stiffly.

182

"Really? You ate two ham and mushroom pizzas on Friday night."

"Who are you, the food police?"

"Just trying to be nice," Mary said, giving them a fake smile. She moved on quickly, crossing the room and finding Trystesse and Hailey who were being harangued by Bernie.

"I have no idea how my phone turned up outside," Hailey was saying to Bernie.

"What do you think the police will find on it?" Bernie asked.

"Um, photos of when I had my nails done? Memes about cats? Honestly, what do you think they're going to find," Hailey said, jabbing a finger towards Bernie's chest.

"We'll know soon enough," Bernie said. For a moment, Mary thought Hailey might give her another slap, but the woman managed to keep hold of her temper.

"Vol au vent? They've got brie in them," Mary said, holding out the tray.

"No thanks," Hailey sniffed. "It's not 1986."

"I'll have one," Trystesse said with a small smile. Mary reckoned she was just taking one to avoid the awkwardness of Bernie and Hailey glaring at each other, but it was still one tick in the 'not pregnant' column.

"Right, well, I better get this back to the table," Mary said.

"Aren't you going to offer me one?" Bernie asked.

183

"Oh. Of course. Here you go."

"Good source of protein, despite the carbs," Bernie said, popping one into her mouth.

"Toodles," Mary said, instantly regretting it. What was it about uncomfortable social situations that turned her into a children's TV presenter?

She put the tray back down on the table, not entirely satisfied with her work. Only Trystesse and Bernie had eaten a vol au vent, but that didn't prove anything except to remove Trystesse from the pregnancy shortlist. Nora, Pru and Hailey could all still be pregnant. And there was no guarantee that the pregnancy had anything to do with the murder either.

Disheartened and lacking anyone to chat with, Mary decided to head for the loo. There was a ladies' toilet just down the corridor and Mary went that way, giving a nod to a police constable as she passed him. It felt like they were being constantly watched, which wasn't particularly pleasant. Also, it made it rather difficult for Mary to sneak off and question anyone. She turned a corner and realised that Nora and Pru were also queueing for what appeared to be a single toilet.

Thinking fast, Mary turned back a few steps before the two women saw her. Thus she would be able to hear what they said without being seen.

"I can't spend one more minute in this place," Pru was saying. "Tryss just spent thirty minutes talking about her Air Fryer. Honestly, I'm going to lose it with her."

Mary, who had recently been eyeing up Air Fryers in the sales, made a mental note never to mention it to the Londoners.

"What about that Mary character? Did you see she was wearing a Barbie necklace? Talk about crimes punishable by death."

The heat started to grow in Mary's cheeks. It was just like at school when the cool girls had made fun of her Superted lunch box. Which, looking back on it, was actually pretty cool and Mary wondered if her mum still had it in her loft. She pressed herself against the wall and tried to listen.

"Their silly Wronged Women's thing... do you think they know who killed Viola?" Nora asked.

Mary held her breath.

"I don't think they have the slightest idea," Pru replied. "But then neither do we, and we were there too."

The breath escaped Mary's mouth with a disappointed 'oof' noise.

"Do you know, I have been wondering lately if... well, I'm probably being silly," Nora said.

"If what?" Pru asked, and Mary found herself mouthing the same question.

"Could it have had something to do with those Newfellow House people?" Nora asked.

Mary frowned. What the hell was Newfellow House?

185

"I don't see how they could have anything to do with it," Pru replied. "And I'd be very careful about mentioning it if I were you. They're notoriously litigious and you don't want to end up in court."

"Yeah, you're right, it was a silly idea," Nora said quickly. "I'm not going to wait here any longer. What kind of crappy hotel only has a single women's toilet? Let's just get back to the food before that fat pregnant one eats it all."

Scurrying backwards a few steps, Mary tried to play it cool when the women came around the corner.

"Hi," she said, giving them a big smile. "Is the loo up here?"

"I wouldn't bother," Pru said, "there's only one so it takes ages. Love your necklace by the way."

Mary gritted her teeth to keep her smile in place. "Thanks," she said.

Chapter 26: Liz

After lunch, Liz had taken the first opportunity to disappear back to her room. Bernie was waving at her from across the room but she pretended not to see. She needed a break, from the case, from Bernie, and from being on her feet.

She propped her swollen ankles up on some pillows, watched mindless telly for a while, and then put in a video call to Dave.

"You've still no idea when you'll be home?" Dave asked, his face a picture of concern.

"Nope," Liz said, popping another shortbread biscuit into her mouth. She had seen a maid's cart when she made her way up to her room and swiped half a dozen of the little packets. "I can't see them letting us out before tomorrow. It's nearly six already."

"I miss you. Sean has been practising his racing skills for when you get back."

Liz grinned. Since her bump had been growing, she had developed a liking for more sedentary activities like her son's computer games.

"Tell him I'm still going to beat him every time."

"I'll tell him. Any news on the murder?"

"The police seem to be waiting for the forensics results before charging anyone. I don't know how they're going to make a case. We were all living together so closely that there probably isn't an inch of that cottage that doesn't have all our DNA all over it."

"You don't know who did it, then?"

"I've got some theories," Liz admitted. "The problem is I think that Bernie, Mary and I all suspect different people. Until we find a real reason why someone might have killed Viola, we're just making guesses. And that's not what the WWC is all about."

"You'll get them in the end," he said, with a husband's loyalty.

"Thanks."

After a few more minutes of chatting she hung up. Tiredness had hit her again, and it wasn't even close to bedtime. She lay on the bed and switched on the hotel telly. It seemed to be set to some channel that showed nothing but reality TV rubbish, but at the moment Liz was finding it quite soothing.

Her phone buzzed and Liz saw she had a text from Mary. Collectively, the WWC had decided to ignore the command from the police officers not to contact each other. Well, Bernie had decided and once she did the other two went along with it.

Have you heard of Newfellow House?

Liz frowned and typed back: *No. Why are you asking?*

She waited while Mary typed out her answer.

188

Pru and Nora were talking about it. Said it might have something to do with Viola's murder. Can't find it online.

Liz went into her internet browser and typed in Newfellow House, but there didn't seem to be any place in Scotland with that name. She clicked down the list of results. There was a Newhamfellow House somewhere in Kent, and a Newfellow foundation, but when she clicked that link it came up not found.

Can't see any relevant results either, Liz sent back. Within a few seconds, Mary replied.

Boo. I'll keep trying. Bernie says can you look into the financial background of all the suspects.

This was more in Liz's wheelhouse. She placed as many pillows as she could find behind her back and settled into work. Her old job had involved sorting through the finances of multi-million pound companies, so it was relatively easy to look into the personal cash flow of the members of the hen-do.

Not all of Liz's methods were strictly speaking legal. If her former employers at the insurance firm had known that she was still using all of her logins, she would be in serious trouble. But like all such firms, no one at the top understood how the IT system worked, so it was relatively easy to subvert it.

Liz wrote down a list of everyone involved in the case, and even though Bernie had asked for the financial details of the suspects, she decided to look into Viola's accounts first. After all, if she had owed someone money, that might be a reason

189

for her murder.

Besides, she knew Viola's address, full name and date of birth, which meant it only took a few minutes before Liz could see her bank details. The credit reference agency Liz was using didn't show her exact numbers, but the presence of several savings accounts that had a minimum of a thousand pounds to open suggested that Viola was doing pretty well.

Next, Liz decided to look into her partner, Alfie. The police seemed to think he had something to do with the murder, despite not being at the cottage. Liz was inclined to side with Bernie that no murderer came from outside the house, but that didn't mean he couldn't have killed Viola through an accomplice.

Alfie Callford's finances were much more complex than his fiancée's. Part of the problem was that he was both the heir and an employee of his parents' estate. To discover how the estate was doing in terms of its solvency would involve several days of work and more resources than Liz had on her laptop. Instead, she took a look at his personal accounts. These were a bit more haphazard, with applications for loans one month, then large investments made another. Alfie might be in trouble, but he had a fairly large cushion behind him if he needed to bail himself out.

Next on the list was Pru Woods. Liz had placed her as a priority due to the letter they had found in her handbag. Sure enough, when Liz did a bit of digging it looked like the company was in trouble. She found a complaint online from a former employee annoyed at being made 'suddenly redundant' just a few weeks ago, and combined with the threat of administration, it suggested that Pru was in real financial difficulties. But why would that make her go after Viola? Maybe she asked Viola for a loan and she refused? It still seemed a little thin for a motive for murder.

Liz checked the time. How could it only be four o'clock? This was the longest Sunday ever. She had noted that none of the police officers had mentioned any hope of them returning home tomorrow. How much longer would she be stuck up here?

She turned the laptop off and shut her eyes. It was time for a little power nap.

Chapter 27: Bernie

It was nearly dinner time and Liz was ignoring Bernie's phone calls. If it wasn't for the police Constable outside, she would have gone around and thumped on her friend's door. Pregnancy was no excuse for slacking on the job, as far as Bernie was concerned. When she was pregnant with her son, she kept working right until her water broke.

Although, even Bernie had to admit to feeling a little fatigued. She had run out of her homemade protein bars and had had to resort to eating the lunch buffet the hotel had provided. She had even accepted a vol au vent for some reason. That was not the attitude that had won her Renfrewshire slimmer of the month three times in a row.

Still, perhaps a little leniency was in order for both Liz and herself. It had been a trying weekend. Bernie was not completely heartless, and she had been friends with Viola. Grief, however, had to take a backseat at least until she worked out who was responsible for the murder. Bernie was taking the whole thing personally. For a murderer to act right under the noses of the WWC was nothing short of an insult.

The musky tang of cigarette smoke tickled Bernie's nose. She went over to the window which she had left open a crack. Sure enough, down below was Howie Callford, puffing away on his death stick.

Acting quickly, Bernie opened the door and walked over to the

Constable. "Can I nip out for a quick smoke?"

"I didn't realise you smoked," the police officer said, his eyes narrowed. "You haven't mentioned it before."

"I know. I only have one every so often. It's the stress, you see."

The Constable rolled his eyes. "Ten minutes, okay? And I'll hear if you try going into any of the other rooms."

Bernie was pleased to hear that her reputation had preceded her. She walked along the corridor, down the stairs and out of a side door.

"Hello," she said when she walked up to Alfie's brother. "I wondered if I could have a quick word."

Howie ground his cigarette into the gravel, even though there was a bin right next to him. "You're working with the police, aren't you?"

"No," Bernie explained. "I'm working for myself. I'm a private investigator. Do you know how much tar is in one of those things, by the way?"

The man just looked at her.

"I wanted to ask you why the police think your brother had something to do with Viola's death."

"Because they're a bunch of muppets," Howie grunted. "Anyone could see that Alfie was obsessed with Viola. He would never hurt a fly."

"What about you? I hear you're not the sort of guy to worry about using your fists."

"Never hit a woman, have I? You can check that with your friends in uniform. I can handle myself, sure, but that's not a crime is it?" He stood back and folded his arms across his chest so that Bernie could see how big his muscles were.

Bernie almost laughed out loud. Howie thought he was a big man, and he was just the sort of man she never had any time for. Working for two decades in the care home meant she saw how that sort of man ended his life, shouting at the nurses and complaining about any change to their routine. Howie thought he was something new, but Bernie reckoned the type was as old as time itself.

"It's a shame you haven't been able to work out recently," Bernie said sweetly.

Howie frowned. "What do you mean?"

"Oh, just that your arms look bigger in this picture." She held up her phone to show a social media page of Howie doing weights in the gym. "I saw this on your page from last month."

The man glared at the phone. "Nah, they're much bigger now. I'm lifting twice a day."

"Sure, sure. Still, you'll be wanting to get back to the gym as soon as you can. I'm a nurse you see. It doesn't take long for all that muscle to turn into fat."

Howie looked a little paler.

"I mean, if we could get this murder all wrapped up then you could get back home. Start working on those biceps again."

The man narrowed his eyes. "I've already told the police that my brother had absolutely nothing to do with all this."

"It is a bit weird though that he came up to Aviemore. You can see why the police think it is suspicious."

Howie shrugged. "It was a stupid mistake. Alfie wanted to surprise Viola. Hailey had told him that they were going out in Aviemore on Saturday night and he thought it would be fun. I told him that no one wants a groom at the hen-do, but he insisted."

"Don't you think that's suspicious?"

"No. You don't know my brother. He was completely infatuated with Viola. I have no idea why. Don't get me wrong, she was all right looking and all that, but he could have got anyone he wanted. Some model or something. I mean, they all threw themselves at him."

"What about you? Do they throw themselves at you?"

Howie laughed. "I do all right. I've got a few on the go right now."

Could he have had a thing for Viola? Bernie thought. It was possible, but murdering your brother's girlfriend because you fancied her seemed a bit of a stretch.

"It's funny you say that, because my friend Mary was in the room when Alfie was interviewed. And she said that you told

195

the police coming up here was your idea. Not Alfie's."

Howie puffed out his cheeks. "Well, maybe I thought it would be a laugh. And I had a bit of a thing going with one of Viola's pals."

"Really? Which one?"

"You can work that out in your own time. You're the private investigator, right? I'm not here to do your job for you." He started to head for the door.

"Who do you think killed her?" Bernie asked.

"One of those jealous bitches on that hen-do. Maybe you, for all I know. When Viola got married to my brother she was going to become rich and famous. Plenty of people would kill for that."

Plenty of shallow people like you, Bernie thought as he turned and left. The police had it wrong, she thought as she made her way back to her room. Howie was much more the type to commit murder than his brother. Once she was back in her room, Bernie opened up her laptop and added Howie Callford to the list of suspects.

Chapter 28: Walker

By seven o'clock in the evening, the sun was setting and the snow had melted into mud-coloured slush on the streets. Walker watched as the odd hardy tourist still made their way along the pavement, looking a little shell-shocked. It was one thing to see Scottish weather in a travel brochure, but quite another to be trapped inside for several days because of it.

The melted snow was settling into dark rust-coloured puddles on the tiled floor of the hotel lobby. A harassed-looking cleaner had put up a bright yellow sign that warned of slipping, and wandered back and forth every few minutes with a mop that merely seemed to spread the water out.

"There are ten more boxes coming," MacLeish said as he walked in the door and handed Walker a cardboard box. This was physical evidence from the cottage, things that weren't part of the immediate crime scene but might be of value. Everything from Viola's room had been taken, along with items from the rest of the house.

MacLeish had a box of his own and they walked up the stairs together.

"Haven't they sent you back down south yet?" MacLeish asked. "I heard the road is open now."

Walker swallowed. "Well, I should probably be going. But I figure that as long as I'm on my own time, Invergryff can't get too mad."

"I think you might be underestimating how petty some officers can be," MacLeish said, but his lips were curled into a smile. "Look, I'm happy to have you here, but you'll have to clear it with the DI. He's just shown up along with the rest of the Murder Investigation Team. They'll be sending me back to the station as soon as we've done the handover."

Walker's hopes fell. Now he would have to make his case for being part of the investigation with a whole new set of officers. He walked into the incident room and looked around for the lead Detective.

A smile spread across his face when he saw who it was.

"Walker! Lord, you get all over the place, don't you? Like the midges in summer," Macleod gave his shoulder a squeeze. "What the hell are you doing in Aviemore?"

"It's sort of a long story," Walker said.

"Tell him about the tank," MacLeish said, giving him a poke in the ribs.

"What tank?"

Twenty minutes later, Walker was happily ensconced as a newly seconded member of the MIT. He knew his bosses back in Invergryff wouldn't be too pleased, but there wouldn't be much they could do about it over the weekend. Besides, they might have the case wrapped up soon enough, Walker thought, even though experience had taught him that murder cases were rarely simple.

"All right lads," Macleod said from the part of the room where they had erected all the whiteboards. "Inspector MacLeish is going to give us all a briefing before we take over."

All the officers, plain-clothed and uniformed, gathered around.

"As you know, we've been fighting the weather on this case. We were only informed of the death of Viola Gordon this morning, although her body was discovered on Saturday morning. There was no phone signal or internet access at the cottage from Friday night, so that is why they are claiming we weren't informed. My team is checking that that was the case. It was Sergeant Walker here that managed to get through to the cottage first thing this morning. He stayed on the scene and the group from the cottage turned up at the station around ten. Once we knew about the deceased, myself and a forensic team went up to the cottage where we conducted preliminary investigations and removed the deceased to the local hospital.

"We're still waiting for most of the forensics, and the post mortem which is being conducted as we speak. But here's what we know. Viola Gordon died sometime between eleven o'clock on Friday night and seven o'clock on Saturday morning. This is confirmed by the witness statements that suggest she was last seen just before two o'clock in the morning when she went up to bed. She was found just before seven. With the roads being closed, it seems more likely that someone in the cottage was best placed to commit murder, but we have some questions about the fiancé. Sergeant Hughson has been looking into him. Graeme, can you give us a summary."

The big bearded man named Graeme Hughson cleared his

throat. "We think Alfie Callford might be worth a hard look. One of my colleagues remembered the name, and there was a bit of a financial scandal a few years ago involving Alfie. He was selling shares in hotels, but the fraud office started to look into it after there were complaints of a Ponzi scheme. The investigation was shut down when Alfie's parents paid off all the bad debt, but he's been on our radar ever since."

"A bit of a stretch from fraud to murder," Macleod said.

Hughson nodded. "Aye, but he's got a reputation for being ruthless. If Viola was some sort of threat to him... There's also the fact that he was up in Aviemore the night she died. Now, if the woman was on her hen-do up here, what the hell was the groom doing skulking around the same area? It's all a bit suspicious."

"Agreed," Macleod tapped the whiteboard next to Alfie's name. "You've already interviewed him, haven't you? What had he to say for himself?"

"Nothing much. Seems to be grieving, but we all know that can be faked. The brother, Howie, is a bit of a loose cannon too. Hell of a temper. He's got a record for a couple of assaults, pub fights, that sort of thing."

"All right, we'll have a good look at them. What about the other suspects?"

MacLeish took over again. "There were seven other women in the house with Viola. Three from Invergryff, two from London, and another two from other parts of Scotland. Any of them would have had the opportunity to kill Viola, but so

200

far there doesn't seem to be any motive. We're hoping the forensics from the bedroom will help us narrow it down."

"Now, we're running out of hours tonight," Macleod said. "I don't want any complaints of ill treatment from our witnesses. I think we should leave the follow up interviews until tomorrow."

"How long can we keep them here?" Walker asked.

"Not that long, unless we place them under arrest. We'll have to rely on their goodwill, but if they want to go home tomorrow, we can't do too much about it."

Walker nodded. He wasn't too sure there was much 'goodwill' about. He suspected most of the women would leave the hotel first thing tomorrow if they could.

Macleod continued the briefing. "MacLeish needs to get back to the station. There's a hell of a lot of clean-up to do after the snows, but he's leaving us half a dozen uniforms to help with the case. Sergeant Hughson here is going to be in charge of sorting through all the physical evidence and making a list of priorities for the techs to have a look at. Sergeant Walker here is on loan from Invergryff for as long as I can manage it, and I want him to take the lead on interviewing our suspects, and that'll start first thing in the morning. Maybe if we can promise to let them away tomorrow afternoon they'll be more likely to co-operate."

A female Constable raised her hand.

"Yes?"

"We've just started to get the first of the fingerprint analysis done. The mobile phone belonging to Hailey Osgold, the one that someone chucked outside in the snow, has come back positive for prints from one of the other women at the cottage."

"Who?"

"Nora Hammond."

Macleod turned to Walker. "Any legitimate reason why her prints would be on her pal's phone?"

"Not that I can think of."

"Then we'll ask her about it first thing in the morning. All right, let's help MacLeish pack up and we'll call it a day. Everyone back here at seven a.m."

Macleod strode over to Walker, who was checking out all the new reports on a free laptop.

"If you speak to reception I'm sure they can sort you out a room," Macleod said. "Unless you'll be heading upstairs to see your girlfriend?"

Walker knew a trap when he saw it. "I think it would be better if I kept my distance, sir, at least until all the interviews have been completed."

The DI grinned. "Good. Now, you get that paperwork finished and get yourself off to bed. No climbing up drainpipes, you hear me?"

"Wouldn't dream of it, sir."

Chapter 29: Mary

Mary woke up at six in the morning on Monday, still fully dressed. She was lying on top of the bed with her laptop on the pillow next to her.

"Ugh," she moaned, rubbing her eyes. She hadn't even taken her make-up off. Last thing she could remember was room service bringing her fish and chips for dinner. She had eaten it, then sat up to make some notes on the case. At some point, she must have passed out.

She stripped off and threw herself into the shower, making sure it was turned up as hot as possible. As the needles of heat dug into her skin, she started to feel a little more alive. What a weekend! Once she was scrubbed clean she wrapped a towel around her hair, put on the hotel robe – always a lovely feeling – and opened the window to release the smell of stale chips.

It was too early to phone Matt and the kids, so she turned on the telly. The hotel wasn't fancy enough to offer streaming, so Mary watched some infomercials. She had just decided to order some microfiber clothes and a fitness DVD when her phone buzzed.

You up? B.

Mary clicked the call button.

"Thank god. Liz isn't answering."

"Bernie, she's pregnant, she'll probably sleep until noon."

"She can sleep on her own time," Bernie grumbled. "I want those financial results. Until we learn anything that suggests otherwise, I'm starting to think that Viola was killed over money."

"I was up late last night looking at the social media stuff," Mary said, which was only half a lie. "There's something a bit weird about Alfie's posts. He keeps talking about manifesting and #blessed, but there are also some random words that come up."

"This Newfellow House that you mentioned?"

"Well, he doesn't use that phrase, as far as I can see. But up until six months ago, he kept mentioning the 'one year plan' and 'life upgrade' and whenever anyone questions him on it, he gets them to private message him. It's like he doesn't want to say too much in public, but at the same time he's posting himself with all these fancy cars and posh hotel rooms so that people want in on the action. It's a little creepy, to be honest with you."

"The police said that they thought he was a con artist, only they couldn't prove it. Sounds like he's up to his old tricks."

"Yeah, but did Viola know about it?" Bernie asked, although Mary knew it was a rhetorical question. "And was she involved?"

"It would explain the fact that she always had plenty of money," Mary replied.

"But she had money before she met Alfie. Unless we've got the dates wrong somehow. I don't know, maths was never my strongpoint. I need Liz to wake up to deal with it."

Mary ignored this comment. "Do you think they will let us go home today?"

"I hope not."

"Really?"

"We'll never get a better chance to solve this case. Every single suspect is right here in the hotel. If we go home we might as well give up."

Mary pinched the bridge of her nose. She was on the verge of what was known amongst her friends as a 'Bernie headache'. "Okay. What do we need to do?"

"I want you to talk to Alfie again. I'm ninety-nine per cent sure it wasn't him that killed Viola, but I want to rule him out for definite."

"Will do."

"I'm going to talk to Hailey again. I still think the fact that she booked the cottage puts her at the top of the suspect list. And there's the whole missing phone thing. I don't suppose Walker mentioned anything about it?"

"No, but I only spoke to him for a couple of minutes last night."

"Well, keep trying! What's the point of having someone on

our team who is shagging the enemy if we can't even get the inside scoop?"

"I'm hanging up now," Mary said, clicking off the call.

Mary did another trawl of social media while she was waiting for breakfast. This time she tried looking up Trystesse MacKinnon. Tryss didn't seem to have much of a social media profile. There was an old account on one of the picture-sharing sites that had a few photos of a younger Tryss at college, but nothing from the last decade. Not to be beaten so easily, Mary looked to see if there was anything else. She eventually found some entries on a farming forum by 'Tryss from Pitlochry' but if an interest in canning meat, making candles and the multiple diseases of sheep were the habits of murderers, then Mary couldn't see the link.

Liz would check out the financial side, but from what Mary could see the woman lived a quiet life on the croft with her husband. There was still the visit to London to investigate, the one where she had had her hair done by Nora, but so far Tryss was at the bottom of Mary's list of suspects. The only thing that marked her apart was the family connection with Viola. Could she be due to inherit something if her cousin died? Mary made a note to ask Bernie if she knew if Viola had made a will.

An hour later there was a knock at the door, and a member of staff informed Mary that the police wanted them all downstairs in the conference room for a meeting, after which breakfast would be served.

On her way into the room, Mary bumped into Liz who had

207

dark circles under her eyes.

"There better be bacon involved or I'm walking," the other woman said.

A young female police officer who looked very nervous walked into the centre of the room.

"Thank you all for coming." The Constable was reading from a piece of paper. "We have completed our initial interviews so we are happy for you to communicate with one another. Over the course of today, we will be looking at options to get you home. We request that you stay patient with us a little longer."

There was an angry murmur at that, but nobody came out and said anything. Bernie would normally be the chief objector to such an abuse of civil liberties, but Mary knew that her desire to see all the suspects kept under lock and key would stop her from saying anything.

Hailey and Trystesse were whispering together in the corner, and Mary walked over to them while the buffet was being set up.

"Bloody cheek," Hailey said to her as she approached. "The police have got nothing on any of us and they expect us to stay here of our own free will.

"I think they're just trying to do their job," Mary replied. "Don't you want Viola's killer caught?"

"I want out of this miserable place. And of course you're going to defend the police. We've heard all about your relationship with Sergeant Walker."

"He's very handsome," Tryss said with a sly smile. "You've done well there."

"Thanks," Mary said, feeling her cheeks grow red.

"You could ask him when the hell I'll be getting my phone back," Hailey said with an angry look.

"I'll ask. I guess they'll give it back once they know it's not connected with the case."

"Why would it?"

"Well, you tell me? Were there any messages between you and Viola that were out of the ordinary?"

The brief pause before Hailey spoke was telling. "Of course not," the woman said. "I'm off to get something to eat."

Mary turned to Trystesse. "Do you know any reason why Hailey's phone might be of interest to the police?"

Tryss looked down at her feet. "I'm not sure I should say."

"It might be important. And the sooner we get to the bottom of all this, the sooner we can get home. I know you want that."

"I think Hailey and Viola were involved in some legal thing. When we were on the train Viola tried to ask her something, but Hailey said she couldn't offer legal advice."

Mary remembered that Bernie had told her Pru had mentioned the same thing. "Do you have any idea what it was about?"

"No, but Viola said it was urgent, so I thought... Well, what with the wedding coming up, I thought it might be something to do with a prenup."

This was news. "Viola wanted a prenup?"

"Or didn't want one. Alfie had all the money, after all, and I thought his parents might be advising one. Then Viola asked Hailey about it from a legal point of view. That's all. So you see, I don't think it had anything to do with the murder."

Satisfied that Trystesse had told her everything there was to know, Mary followed her nose to the buffet table where a tray of bacon had arrived.

Liz was stuffing a well-fired roll with mounds of glistening bacon just as Mary arrived with her plate.

"Do you know Bernie started calling me at six this morning?" Liz said, through a mouthful of her roll.

"Oh yes. She called me too."

"You weren't stupid enough to answer, were you?" Liz saw Mary's face and chuckled. "I never answer Bernie if she phones before eight. It only encourages her."

"I'll know for next time. She's dying for those financial records."

"I know. She accosted me about them a minute ago. I should have most of them done by the end of today. Look out, she's coming back out of the kitchen. She went to complain about the breakfast and see if she could get anything that wasn't fried."

Mary looked down at her plate of bacon, square sausage, eggs and tattie scone. "I'm away around the corner before she can ruin this for me."

Tucked away out of sight of her boss, Mary was able to enjoy her fry-up in peace. And it was joyous indeed. She didn't normally have a cooked breakfast at home, because there was hardly the time with the kids clamouring for toast and cereal as soon as they got up, but she greatly enjoyed one when she got the chance. Even though she would be suffering from heartburn later, it was still worth it.

Once she had finished her delicious breakfast, Mary went down to Reception, partly to ask if she could have more tea and shortbread in her room, but mainly to see if she could accidentally bump into Walker.

As she came down the stairs she was surprised to see Nora and Pru standing at the desk with their suitcases beside them. There were no police officers in sight, and they were asking the woman at the desk to phone them a taxi.

"Are you leaving?" Mary asked them.

"I bloody well hope so," Nora said. Her phone rang as she stepped to one side to answer it.

"We're going to see about getting out of here today," Pru said, giving her suitcase a kick when the wheels got stuck in the carpet. "Nora and I were chatting last night and we don't think they can legally make us stay. There's a train down south in a

211

couple of hours and we're going to be on it."

"Aren't you worried that makes you look a bit suspicious?"

"No. In fact, I couldn't care less what a bunch of Highland coppers think about me."

Nora clicked off her call and the two women went through the revolving door to wait for their taxi. After a few moments of thought, Mary texted Walker.

Nora and Pru leaving hotel.

She clicked send. Never before had Mary felt like such a narc. She didn't even really understand what a narc was, but snitching on the women to her cop boyfriend made her feel like she was probably worthy of the term.

Just a few seconds later, two police constables arrived and started arguing with the women. Mary slunk away before they noticed her watching them. She would never be one of the cool girls now, Mary thought sadly. And she hadn't even had a chance to refill the shortbread.

Chapter 30: Liz

It wasn't long after breakfast that Liz had a knock at her hotel room door and opened it to let an agitated Mary Plunkett inside.

"Nora and Pru were trying to leave but I've dobbed them into the police," the other woman said, her words coming out in a rush.

"Did they stop them?"

"I hope so. Bernie will be hopping mad if they let two of our best suspects leave."

"Talking about the police, should you even be here?"

"They're letting us talk to each other now that they've done all the initial interviews. I think Bernie had a go at some of the young PCs and they ended up giving in."

Liz couldn't help but laugh. "The usual Bernie tactic, then. I've just got off the phone with her. I've found Newfellow House."

"Great," Mary said. "Where is it?"

Liz shook her head. "It's not a place, it's a company. Or it was. I found it on the Companies House website where people have to list their businesses. It was formed five years ago and went into administration just last year."

"Okay, so how does it connect back to Viola?"

"I'm not sure. But I've found the directors of the company, Neil Cook and Riccarda Fawcett. They both live in Edinburgh, according to the business listing. I'm going to look a bit closer at them and the company itself. The website is gone and there's not much left online about it. And that in itself is a bit fishy: normally with a company that had closed down that recently there would be something still on the internet. I did find a few reviews on social media, and they're seriously weird."

"In what way?"

"Well, there's plenty of five-star reviews, saying that Newfellow House 'changed my life' and that the seminars were 'transformational'. From what I can gather, it was some sort of consultancy business. Seminars are mentioned quite a lot, as well as 'mentoring', but details are thin on the ground. Then there are the bad reviews."

Liz held up her phone so that Mary could read them.

This is a SCAM. Do not believe the hype, one said. Another was a long rant that seemed almost overly personal.

Don't let them into your life. Newfellows took away everything I had. Don't trust them. They're a bunch of backstabbers and instead of the Road to Success it's the Road to Disaster.

"Wow. Strong stuff for a consultancy firm. It almost sounds more like a cult."

"Or one of these pyramid schemes," Liz said. "You know, like the ones trying to get you to buy expensive make-up and sell it to your friends."

"Ugh. Or candles. I always get people messaging me about candles. And I don't even have flames in the house since that time Peter set his socks on fire."

"Bernie wants me to go back through all the suspects and find out if anyone other than Viola had a connection to the place. I don't suppose Nora and Pru said if Viola was a victim of the scam, or one of the scammers?"

"No. They just mentioned the name."

"Okay," Liz said, rubbing the small of her back. "I'll keep checking."

"I'm off to see if I can find Walker. He's not replying to my texts which makes me think the police might be onto something and he can't tell me about it yet. Bernie will be so mad if they find the killer before we do."

Liz tilted her head to one side. "You need to stop worrying about what makes Bernie mad. She's not really that scary."

"You tell yourself that," Mary said darkly, then left to track down her boyfriend.

Just when Liz thought she might get a few moments of peace, her phone rang.

"Hello. It's Fiona Omoregie from the school."

"Oh, hi, thanks so much for getting back to me."

"I didn't think you would get in touch, considering last time you were here you used my login without my permission and accessed confidential files."

"Ah," Liz was hoping the woman wouldn't bring that up. "In fairness, it was for a murder case. Without that information, we would never have found out who killed one of your teachers."

"I'm very busy, Liz, what is it."

Liz took a deep breath. "You'll have heard about Viola Gordon?"

"Yes. Dreadful. Did you know she was about to get married?"

"I was on the hen night."

There was an intake of breath on the other end of the phone. "So you were there when it happened?"

"Near enough. Look, I need your help with something."

"Just like last time?"

"I'm not trying to cause you any trouble, I promise. But one of the people here killed Viola, and I need some information to find out who it was."

"I'm not promising to answer, but you can ask your questions if you want."

Liz grinned. "All right. What I'm trying to work out is why Viola was working in the school at all. From what I can see,

216

she had plenty of other money from investments and property and so on. What I can't work out is why she would take such a low paid job. Did she want to be a teacher one day?"

"No. In fact, and I don't say this lightly, I don't think she even liked kids that much. Look, you can't let this come out in the papers, okay?"

"I promise."

"The school were thinking about firing her. In fact, she had a disciplinary meeting lined up for the week she came back."

"What did she do?"

"She'd been... I don't know how to describe it, but she had been sort of recruiting from the parents. She had all these schemes like making your own candles, selling beauty products, even cryptocurrency, although she never seemed that good at maths. We were starting to get complaints from the parents that Viola was getting them to sign up to these things and then ignoring them when things went wrong. Which, as I'm sure you'll understand, always happens with these sorts of things."

Liz had heard enough. It explained exactly what Viola was up to at the school, along with the sources of her mysterious income. "Thanks, Fiona."

"Feel free never to call me again, Liz," the other woman said and hung up the call.

Just great, Liz thought as she wiggled her swollen feet. I'll be getting a reputation like Bernie for my sparkling social interaction.

217

Chapter 31: Bernie

It wasn't the first time Bernie had been threatened with arrest, and it wouldn't be the last.

"I just want to know what's going on?" she repeated to Detective Inspector Macleod for the third time. "I saw a police van pull up outside, then leave again in ten minutes. That suggests to me that you've taken someone to the station. I just want to know who it was.

"And I want you to know that if you take up any more of my time, I will have you arrested for obstructing a police investigation."

Perhaps she was pushing her luck just a tiny bit, Bernie thought as she watched the DI drive off in his car. But her spidey senses were telling her that something had happened in the police investigation. The officers that were still at the hotel seemed cheerier, as if they had made some progress.

That, sadly, was more than Bernie had. She stomped up the stairs, thinking she would call in on Liz when her phone started buzzing. She pulled it out of her pocket. It was an unknown number. Half expecting it to be a junk call, Bernie answered it.

"Is that Bernie Paterson?" A voice whispered.

"Yes. Who is it?"

"It's Nora. From the hen-do."

Bernie puffed out a surprised breath. She hadn't even known the woman had her number. It wasn't like they had hit it off.

"Why are you calling me?" Bernie asked bluntly.

"Because I'm in deep trouble. I've just been arrested for Viola's murder."

"What?"

"Yeah. The police have stuck me in the back of their van, but they don't know I've still got my work phone on me. I got your number from your Wronged Women's Co-operative website. The cops are standing outside waiting for orders, I guess, so I don't have long. Listen, is it true that you're actually a decent private investigator?"

"Of course it's true."

"Then I want to employ you. I want you to prove I'm innocent."

Bernie tapped her fingers on the window. "Are you sure I'm the best person to do that?"

"Look, I think you're a cold bitch, but that's just the sort of person I need to sort through all this crap. Someone is fitting me up for this, and you were at the cottage. You know how it was and you're not going to be fooled by all the sweet talking like the police were."

"Why do they think you did it?"

"Because of the money," Nora hissed. "Because Viola cost me

all my savings, and then some. So they think I went and murdered her."

"But you didn't?"

"No! Me and Pru had it out with her that Friday night. It was all to do with the Newfellow House thing and then... Crap."

There was a male voice in the background, then the call cut off. Bernie thought about calling Nora back, but surely that would only get her in more trouble.

Immediately, Bernie opened up a group chat with Mary and Liz.

Nora arrested for murder. Wants us to investigate. New client. £,£,£. B.

Mary messaged back straight away. It was a shocked emoji character with the hands over its mouth.

What if she is guilty? Liz typed.

Non-refundable client deposit. Bernie wrote, then added. *If she's guilty then we can't do any more. But until then we'll go back over all the other suspects. And we need to move fast. Police are taking her to the station right now.*

I'll speak to Pru, Mary wrote. *She might give us more info now that her friend has been arrested.*

I'm nearly finished on the list of financial information for each suspect, Liz added. *I'll send it over in the next hour.*

Bernie gave Finn a quick call just to check that there were no dramas at home. Ewan had recently been struggling to get up in the mornings for school, and Bernie was keeping an eye on it to see if it was going to turn into a problem. Finn informed her that he had gone in fine that morning and that Witch the cat had brought in not one but two mice as presents.

When she hung up the call Bernie had to shake off a feeling of homesickness. Mary and Liz might think her heartless, but that was far from the truth. She just saved her emotions for when it was really needed. Just like the others, she was missing home, but she knew that she had a job to do in Aviemore.

It was time to get tough. With Nora being arrested, the chief suspects remaining in the hotel were Pru, Hailey and Trystesse. Mary was going to tackle Pru, and Bernie was waiting until she heard what was on the mobile phone before she cornered Hailey. This way of thinking meant that five minutes later she was knocking on Trystesse's hotel room door.

"I'm on the phone," Trystesse said, her mobile in her hand.

"I can wait while you hang up," Bernie said, pushing past her into the room. She was somewhat affronted to see that the room was larger than her own, with a chair in the window. Bernie sat down and waited.

"Talk to you later," the other woman said and hung up with an irritated expression.

"You've heard about Nora?"

Tryss nodded. "Hailey was there when they took her in. She was making a bit of a scene, by all accounts."

"Well, you would, wouldn't you? If you were innocent?"

"I suppose so." Tryss had a tube of handcream that she was rubbing into her palms. "It's working on the croft," she said when she noticed Bernie watching her. "My hands chap something terrible."

"I was the same at the care home," Bernie said. "All that hand washing dries out the skin. I recommend beeswax."

"Thanks," Tryss said. "Do you think now that Nora has been arrested, they'll let us go home?"

"Only if they charge her," Bernie said. "While she's in custody I'm trying to tie up any loose ends. I wanted to ask you about your trip to London."

Tryss looked surprised. "How do you know about that?"

Bernie ignored the question. "I was surprised that you had been down there, because I had the impression at the hen-do that you hadn't met the London girls before."

"Well, I think we all wanted to forget about it, to be honest. Viola had persuaded me to go down. I'm a big fan of musicals, and she'd booked us in to see Phantom. Ever seen it?"

"Can't stand musicals. People singing their hearts out about the silliest situations. They're all dreadful," Bernie replied.

"Right. We were only in London for the one night, but Viola had arranged that we would get our nails done beforehand. She took me to Nora's salon to get my hair and nails done, then we met Pru for a drink. They had chosen this super posh

222

cocktail bar that was twenty quid a drink. I've never felt more out of place. I could see that they were talking about me, just like they were at the cottage. They were a right bunch, the lot of them."

"You seemed to get on okay with Hailey?"

"I sort of had to as we were sharing a room for the hen-do. But she was just as bad as the others. Perfectly nice to my face, then slagging me off once my back was turned."

"Why do you think Viola was friends with them?"

Tryss laughed. "She might be dead, but my cousin was no saint either. No, they were perfectly well-suited. Bunch of slags the lot of them. In fact... well, I wouldn't like to gossip."

Bernie could have shaken the woman. "It's a murder investigation, not gossiping in the school playground. You can't hold anything back that might be relevant to the case."

"Okay. Well, when I was down in London that time, after we went to the musical there was a party at Alfie's flat."

"I didn't realise he lived in London?"

"He doesn't, not full time anyway. But the family is loaded, so him and his brother have what they were calling a 'bolthole'. It was a flat in Chelsea that is bigger than my house! Anyway, I didn't want to go, but I got dragged along to a party there. Afterwards, we were all meant to be staying at Nora's place because it was nearby, but Pru never left. She snuck in early in the morning, and I don't think the others realised, but she definitely spent the night at Alfie's place."

223

This was news. "You think they were having an affair?"

"No! Or at least, I don't think so. But maybe on that night... Viola never mentioned it, and neither did I, so I don't think she knew. I shouldn't have said anything."

Tryss looked miserable. Bernie patted her arm, even though comforting people was not her strong point.

"Thank you for telling me. It's probably nothing, but it's important that we don't have any secrets where Viola's murder is concerned."

Tryss just kept her head bowed. After a little more awkward small talk, Bernie let herself out of the room. She needed to phone Mary before she spoke to Pru.

Chapter 32: Walker

It wasn't until after she was already in custody that Walker found out Nora had been arrested. As Macleod explained, it had all happened quickly.

"Viola's phone turned up," the Detective Inspector told him. "We found it hidden in the living room at the cottage. Someone had slipped it inside a DVD of *Pretty Woman*. And that someone, when we did a fingerprint match, was Nora Hammond. The Constable that found that phone deserves a promotion. It didn't take the techs too long to get into it, and then we found the messages from Nora. She had deleted them from her own phone, but it's clear that she was getting more and more annoyed with Viola over the last few months. She kept asking about money and investments, and Viola seemed to be fobbing her off. In the last message, Viola promised to explain it all at the hen-do."

"What were these investments?"

"We're not too sure yet, but it might not be a coincidence that Viola's fiancé is a certified conman. Maybe they were pulling a scam together on Nora and it backfired. We've got our forensic accountants working on it now, but we had enough to arrest her today. Plus, with her heading back down south, we were worried she was a flight risk."

Walker couldn't disagree with that. Besides, if they had let the woman leave Scotland it would have made things infinitely trickier as they would have had to liaise with the Metropolitan police, and that would have slowed everything down.

It had put pressure on the investigation, however. The custody clock was now ticking and it was imperative that they got all their evidence lined up before twenty-four hours had passed, after which point they would have to either charge or release the woman.

Walker grabbed a spare laptop and caught up on the investigation so far. The forensics on the physical evidence was starting to come in. It was confirmed that the pillowcase had been the means of asphyxiation as fibres from it had been found in Viola's mouth and nose.

He had just finished reading through the report – he always made sure to read every document twice – when his phone buzzed.

You didn't tell me you arrested Nora, Mary had sent him, then followed it up with an angry gif of one of the orcs from Lord of the Rings snarling and waving a sword.

Didn't know. Besides, not meant to tell you anything, Walker wrote back. He thought for a few seconds then softened it with two kisses. *Xx.*

He didn't get to see if he replied because he was offered a space in a squad car to the station to watch Nora get questioned by DI Macleod.

For this interview, held in the Aviemore police station, Walker was not invited into the room. He was, after all, still an outsider. Instead, the interview was conducted by Macleod with Sergeant Hughson in tow. Walker was, however, allowed to watch from behind the mirrored glass.

MacLeish was watching with him. "You're very quiet," he said to Walker while they waited for Nora to be brought into the interview room.

"I'm not sure we've got this one right, sir," Walker said, voicing the doubt that had been growing since they had picked the woman up.

"You don't think she killed her friend?"

"I just don't see what she had to gain. Yes, Viola led her into some bad investments, but I don't see that as a motive for murder. Or rather, no worse than Pru, who was in the same position."

"I disagree," MacLeish said. "According to our financial experts, 'Luxury by Eleanora' is in all kinds of trouble. Nora has been borrowing from the business to pay off her personal debts, and these appear to be connected to the money she invested with Viola over the last year. She could be about to lose her business. Plenty of people have killed for that."

Their discussion was interrupted by the arrival of Nora in the interview room. If Walker had thought she was going to be upset and frightened, then he had underestimated the woman. She walked in with a straight back and an air of indignation. She had been offered a solicitor, but had turned it down.

Once the usual formalities of identification were over, Sergeant

227

Hughson took the lead in asking the questions. He started by getting Nora to confirm the timeline of the night Viola was killed, then he started asking about their relationship.

"We know that you sent several messages to Viola over the last few months regarding financial transactions." Hughson slid a printout of the text message exchange across the desk. "Can you tell us what this was about?"

"Viola owed me some money, and she was avoiding talking about it. It was no big deal," Nora said, flicking her hair out of her face. "She said she would sort it out at the hen-do."

"And did she?"

Nora paused. "We hadn't had a chance to talk about it before she died."

"Well that is unfortunate," Macleod said. "We've had a look at your accounts. It seems that you've been borrowing against the business."

She looked down at her nails. "That's right. But we're coming up to the busy season. It'll be tough, but I'll pay it all back over the next few months."

MacLeod leaned back in his chair. "Your friend Pru was in debt as well. Perhaps the two of you were working together."

"Pru had nothing to do with this either. Look, I wanted the money from Viola, that's true. But how would killing her get me anything?"

"Let's leave that to one side for a moment," MacLeod said,

228

changing his tactics, "I'm trying to understand why you would invest money with someone who worked as a school secretary? Surely that was taking a risk?"

"Viola was just a middle-man," Nora said. "She was working for this company, Newfellow House. They had these seminars that showed you how you could make more money, sort of entrepreneurial stuff. Viola introduced me and Pru to loads of people that had made money with them. We thought... it seemed legit."

"But it wasn't?"

"We got some money back straight away, but less than what we put in. Then when we asked to see the accounts where the money was invested, they got cagey. They said part of the money was non-refundable, that it had gone into our 'coaching' or whatever. It was Pru that realised it was a scam at first. I guess I didn't want to believe that I had been so stupid as to trust them."

"Why did you go after Viola for the money if she was just an agent for this Newfellow House place?"

"Because she was in it up to her eyeballs. She recruited for them, got suckers like us to join up. And she knew fine well what was going on."

"That must have been a terrible betrayal."

Nora's lip was trembling by now. "Yes, it was... but I still didn't kill her! We were going to sort it all out this weekend."

The woman was getting agitated, so Macleod went in for the

229

kill. He took a piece of paper out of the file in front of him and slid it across the table.

"This is a forensic analysis of trace evidence on the pillow that we believe was used to smother Viola Gordon. If you see this compound here, and the picture of the tiny flakes of colour, it shows that we found an exact match for your nail polish."

"My... that can't be right. I never touched the pillow."

"The science suggests otherwise."

Nora folded her arms. "I want to speak to a solicitor. Now."

MacLeish walked towards the door. "That's us for a few hours until we can get the duty solicitor. I'll get one of the lads to give you a lift back to the hotel. All of our tanks are busy today."

"Thanks," Walker said. He ignored the comment. After all, he was not going to live that one down any time soon.

Chapter 33: Mary

Mary had been back in her room for a couple of hours before she realised that she had bacon grease on her top. She hoped no one else at breakfast had noticed. Mind you, after what they had been through in the last few days, it was hardly something to worry about. She pulled off her top, put it in the sink to soak and rooted around in her suitcase for something to wear.

There was a furious knocking at the door. Worried that something was wrong, Mary pulled the hotel robe over her bra and jeans and opened the door a crack.

Bernie barrelled into the room, dragging Liz behind her.

"Christ, Bernie, I was getting changed," Mary said, pulling the robe around herself more tightly.

"That doesn't matter," Bernie said, with her usual concern for the comfort of others, "I've got something important to tell you. We've got a new client."

"We've got a new case? I didn't realise we had finished this one."

"We haven't. Our new client is Nora Hammond."

Mary frowned, trying to get her head around what was going on. "Sorry, our new client is the person that has just been arrested for Viola's murder?"

"Who better? She's got a good reason to pay the bill." Bernie flung herself down on Mary's bed. "Now we need to work out what the police have got on her. Any news from your boyfriend?"

"I'm not sure we've quite defined our relationship in those terms yet," Mary said stubbornly. She knew it would annoy Bernie but the hotel wasn't that warm and she could feel a draft moving up her robe.

"Well, he called you his girlfriend," Bernie said.

"Did he?" Mary grinned.

"Yes. Can we get on with the brutal murder now?"

"Okay," Mary said, still smiling. "Where do you want us to start?"

Bernie stood up and started to pace around the room. "Liz, I need you to go over Nora and Viola's financial links with a fine tooth comb. If the police think money was the motive, we need to prove them wrong. Or, we need to prove that the money was more of a problem for our other suspects."

"Are we still just looking at Hailey, Pru and Trystesse for the other possible killers?" Liz asked.

"Yes. Although we're not going to discount Alfie as an outside chance. Now, I happened to be walking past the incident room earlier, and they had a list of the physical evidence connecting Nora to Viola's body. The main things were her nail polish on the pillowcase and her fingerprints on Viola's phone."

232

"They found Viola's phone?"

"Looks like it. Turns out your search wasn't that thorough after all," Bernie said with a sniff.

"Now you wait a minute –" Liz took a step towards Bernie, her hands on her hips.

"Let's just focus on what we have to do now, shall we?" Mary said. "And how the hell did you get all this information, Bernie? There's no way you just overheard it."

Bernie smiled. "I bribed the cleaner to take a photo of the whiteboard for me for twenty quid."

Mary decided it was probably best not to tell Walker about that one.

"Now, I'm not sure about the nail polish, we might have to ask Nora about that, but for the moment I want to focus on Viola's phone. If Nora's fingerprints are on it, then I want to know why she took it. I want you, Mary, to talk to Pru about it today. See if she knows why Nora had the phone in the first place."

"All right," Mary said, even though she was still a teeny bit scared of the uber-fashionable Pru. She would probably have to wear something other than jeans and a hotel bathrobe.

Bernie and Liz left, bickering as they went. Mary sorted through her suitcase until she found a black tunic-style top that was at least free from bacon stains. She added some big hooped gold earrings, because they made her happy and she felt she needed a bit of a lift before facing one of the Mean

233

Girls.

Mary consulted her list of room numbers that Bernie had somehow obtained from the hotel staff and discovered that Pru was on the floor above her. She walked to her room and knocked on the door.

"Yes?" Pru, always skinny, had a gaunt look about her face. Mary wondered if she'd had any sleep at all in the last few days.

"Would it be okay to come in?"

"I'm just packing up," Pru said, making no move out of the doorway. "I'm kind of busy."

"I heard about Nora. She's asked the WWC to look into her case. We're going to prove her innocence."

Pru stared for a moment, then stifled a yawn. "I suppose you better come in then."

The stale smell of tobacco and the open window showed that Pru was ignoring the no smoking status of the hotel. Mary wrinkled her nose but said nothing, making sure to take the chair closest to the open window.

Once she had moved a pile of clothes to one side, Pru sat down on the bed.

"How long will they keep Nora for?" she asked.

"It depends on what they decide to do. They've got twenty-four hours to question her, then they either charge her with the murder or they let her go."

"They'll have to let her go. She didn't do anything."

Mary gave her a sharp look. "Are you sure about that?"

"Yes."

"It seems to me like you both had a pretty solid motive. Viola owed you money, didn't she?"

Pru gasped. "How do you know that?"

"Liz is some kind of financial wizard. She looked into your accounts, and Viola's. There was money going back and forth, but more of it went to Viola than came back to you two. And we know that your business is in trouble."

"It was this Newfellow House business," Pru said, taking a deep breath. "It all started with some simple investments. At first, we made money. They showed us how to work out all our business taxes so that we saved cash. Then Viola pushed us to become 'gold members'. It meant we had these networking sessions with business coaches. At the time it all sounded amazing, and they had all the recommendations, celebrity clients, the works. But pretty soon it started to unravel. When Nora and I tackled Viola about the money, she just said she was the middle-man. Like, she made the introductions, but it had been our choice to invest. Which was half true, I guess."

"And you must have been pretty mad about that, right? You and Nora?"

"Of course. But not enough to kill her. Look, I'm just as upset as anyone that Viola's dead, but she was playing a

235

dangerous game. If it wasn't for her introducing us to Newfellow House, me and Nora would still have all our money. I know that we didn't kill her, but I'm not surprised that someone else did."

"Were Hailey or Trystesse involved in Newfellow House?"

"Not as far as I know, although sometimes I wondered if Hailey knew about it. Whenever we brought it up with Viola, Hailey would make sure she left the room."

She hated to think it, but Mary was starting to believe that Bernie might have been wrong to take the case from Nora. So far, she still looked like the most likely suspect, and nothing Pru had said had changed that.

"Why did you take Viola's phone? Was there something on there you didn't want the police to see?"

"We didn't take Viola's phone."

"Then why were Nora's fingerprints all over it?"

"No. That can't be right. She never took Viola's phone. She only took Hailey's."

Mary raised an eyebrow. "Nora took Hailey's phone?"

Pru's mouth turned down at the corners. "We were worried that the police would think we had something to do with Viola's death, because of all the money stuff. I guess we thought it would be better if the attention was on Hailey."

"You were framing her?"

"No! Nothing that bad. We just thought… well, we thought if we dropped enough hints that there was trouble with Hailey then you would go after her and stop looking at us."

"So you made up the thing about the 'legal stuff' with Viola?" Mary said, remembering that Bernie had made a note about it on the spreadsheet.

"No, it wasn't made up at all. I really did see them having this like, totally intense discussion on the train. But then I knew once you realised that Nora and I were both scammed out of our money you would blame it all on us. So Nora took Hailey's phone because we thought it would look like she was trying to get rid of it. I thought it was a pretty clever idea."

Mary resisted the urge to say how stupid they had been. "Only now that the police have arrested Nora it's going to look even worse when they discover she was trying to frame someone else."

"Oh bollocks, I never meant for that to happen. I've just… I've got so much on my plate right now, and so does Nora. Neither of us was thinking straight."

Mary had a hunch and decided to go with it. "And it's hard to think straight when you find out you're pregnant, isn't it?"

One look at Pru's face told her she had hit the jackpot.

"I don't… What do you mean?"

"You are pregnant, aren't you?"

"How did you work it out?" Pru said, curling her knees up to

237

her chest and wiping her eyes.

"Well, I found a packet of pregnancy vitamins in the cottage. And then you didn't eat the vol au vents."

"The what?"

Mary shrugged. "It doesn't matter. It wasn't too hard to work out. I am an investigator after all."

"I suppose you are. You won't tell anyone, will you?"

"Only if it's relevant to the case," Mary said, which was a roundabout way of saying 'maybe'.

"I don't want anyone to know, because of who the father is."

Mary took a deep breath. "It's Alfie, isn't it? We know that you spent that weekend at his place."

Pru put her hand to her mouth. "Alfie? You think I was shagging Viola's fiancé? Of course it's not bloody Alfie."

"Oh," Mary sat back, momentarily confused. "Then who is the father?"

"It's Alfie's brother, Howie."

"Ah." That explained why she had been at the flat, just like Tryss had told them. Alfie and Howie lived together.

"But why were you so worried about people finding out?" Mary said, trying to get it all straight in her head. "Howie's not engaged to anyone, is he?"

"No, but he's a total prick." Pru sniffed. "I didn't want anyone to know that I'd been stupid enough to get pregnant by such an arrogant dick."

Mary could hardly argue with that. She patted Pru on the arm. "You know, plenty of people get pregnant by dicks. Um. If you know what I mean. I thought my kids' dad was a great guy, right up until he gambled all their savings away and left us destitute."

"Thanks. Really, I shouldn't keep the baby at all. That would be the logical decision, right? Only I'm nearly forty and this might be my last chance. And I'm already... well, I've sort of fallen in love with the little thing. I've cut right back on the ciggies, only having one a day now, and maybe I'll manage to stop that soon. And the kid's only got a fifty per cent chance of growing up a prick, right?"

"I'd say a better chance than that," Mary replied with a smile. "Can I ask, did Viola know about the pregnancy?"

Pru shook her head. "No. She would have done her nut about it. She knew I'd had a bit of a thing with Howie, and she didn't like it at all. If I'd told her I was pregnant, especially before the wedding, she would probably have thought I was trying to steal her thunder or something. She was obsessed with that bloody wedding. I wasn't even going to go."

"You weren't?"

"No. I'd have to see Howie again, wouldn't I? But Nora said I should go, that it would look more suspicious if I didn't."

"Nora knew about the baby?"

"She was the first one I told." Pru looked up from a crumpled tissue. "She said not to worry about it. That she would help out with the nappies and the childcare and everything. And now she's going to be in prison. So I'll be on my own. Again."

"Do you think Nora killed Viola?"

"No. The thing is, I was there that night. Yes, we had some words with Viola about the money, but she said she was going to sort it all out. And we had a good old bitching session slagging her off when she went up to bed. But that was it."

Mary leaned forward. "But you can't say for definite that Nora didn't go into her room that night, can you?"

Pru shook her head and said nothing.

"Is there anything else you can tell me?" Mary asked, sensing it was time to go. "It might just help your friend prove her innocence."

"And maybe I just give you a really good reason to lock her up," Pru said, her hands balled into fists. "You need to leave. Now."

Chapter 34: Liz

The hotel reception was the only part of the building that still had a little of the Victorian grandeur left with its sweeping oak staircase that led to the upper floors. The reception desk itself was a nasty plastic affair behind which two women in their sixties were comparing pictures of their grandchildren.

Liz checked her watch. Bernie was running late, which was unlike her. She hoped she wasn't getting into mischief. Or, if she was, then it was the sort of mischief that would help them solve the case. A twinge in her back reminded Liz that she had spent far too much time sitting on the bed in her room working on her laptop. She had hoped that she might manage a quick swim in the hotel pool, if Bernie didn't take too long interrogating her about the financial information she was passing on.

While she was waiting, Liz saw an older couple walk up to Reception. They were dressed like something out of *Monarch of the Glen*, the white-haired man in full-on tweeds, the woman in a very expensive designer dress and cashmere coat that would have looked better on someone with curves.

They were met at the desk by one of the young female Constables and they immediately started giving her the third degree. Liz couldn't quite hear what they were saying over the terrible elevator music that was pumped out of the hotel speakers.

At that moment Hailey walked past, and Liz grabbed her arm.

"Any idea who those people are that are giving the police officers a hard time?"

"Those are Alfie's parents," Hailey said, peering out of the window. "Well, his dad and his new step mum. They're 'new money', even though his dad likes to refer to their place as Callford House. Iain Callford, that's his name and the wife is Ricky something or other. Short for Riccarda, she's Italian."

Riccarda. Why did that ring a bell?

"Not Riccarda Fawcett?"

"That was her name before she remarried. Viola used to love gossiping about her. She's on her third rich husband and every divorce has made her more money than the last."

"Well, that is interesting."

"Is it?" Hailey frowned. "Look, can't you stop all this investigating nonsense now? They've arrested Nora so there's a chance we might be able to go home and get on with our lives. Don't you want that?"

"Not if it wasn't Nora that killed Viola," Liz said firmly. "I'm not about to let a murderer go free."

"I think they've caught the murderer," Hailey said, crossing her arms. "I never liked those London girls. They were always slagging me off behind my back. I'm glad she's going to spend the rest of her life in prison. It's exactly what she deserves."

242

Hailey was about to leave when Liz touched her shoulder.

"I've been meaning to ask you," she said. "Did you ever sort out the prenup situation with Viola?"

"Prenup? Do you mean for Viola and Alfie? They didn't have a prenup."

"She didn't ask your advice on it?"

"No. And it's hardly my area of expertise. This is the first I've heard they were even considering one. Where on earth did you get that idea from?"

"From Tryss. She says she overheard you arguing about some sort of legal advice with Viola."

"Oh, that. No that was… more of a financial nature. And I told her I couldn't give her any advice anyway, not without risking my own position."

"Let me guess," Liz said. "It was about some not entirely kosher investment schemes."

Hailey's hands balled into fists. "I can't talk about it. And I told Viola I wanted absolutely nothing to do with any of it. I wouldn't risk my career for her bad decisions, that's for sure."

Before Liz could say anything else, Hailey hurried back up the stairs. Liz returned to watching the couple at the desk. Riccarda Fawcett, former director of Newfellow House was married to Alfie's father. That had to be significant.

She pulled out her phone and rang Bernie. "Where are you?"

"I'm trying to get DI MacLeod to see me. I've been waiting for ages."

Liz rubbed her back. The problem with Bernie was that she was very good at bullying people into talking to her. The issue came when someone stood up to her, she simply refused to back down. "He's not going to tell you anything about the case, you know."

"I don't expect him to. But I'm going to tell him something, and then he'll have a reason to give me some information in return. I'm going to tell him everything we found out about Newfellow House."

"Everything *we* found out?"

"Was that a certain tone in your voice?"

"No, no, not at all. Listen, on that subject, I've just found something else that connects everything. You know how we thought that Viola was working for Newfellow House in some capacity? Well, it's more complicated than that. I've just seen Alfie's stepmother and her name is Riccarda Callford, but it used to be Riccarda Fawcett."

"Should that mean something to me?"

Liz sighed. "If you're going to use my research for bribery, you might as well read it. She was one of the founders of Newfellow House."

"Wow. That is news. What does that mean for the case?"

"I'm not sure yet, but it ties Alfie and his family into all this dodgy investment stuff. Might be worth a chat with him."

"Excellent. His room is on the fourth floor."

"I didn't mean it should be me to talk to him."

"Why not? You can dazzle him with your financial prowess. Call me back when you're done."

Liz decided to take the lift to the fourth floor. When Alfie opened the door to her he looked a little better than he had the day before. Still shattered, but not quite as disconnected as before.

"Hi," he said. "Can I help you?"

"Sorry to bother you. I was wondering if we could have a bit of a chat about the investigation."

Alfie nodded, opening the door to let her in. It was all too miserable for words. The last time she had spoken to him was when they had told him Viola was dead. Being part of the Wronged Women's Co-operative meant you often had to do distasteful things, but harassing people who were in this sort of state wasn't Liz's idea of a good day at work.

"Did the police inform you about Nora?"

"Yes."

"Well, we're not too sure that she did it. Me, Bernie and Mary that is."

"Why not?"

Because she's a paying client and Bernie doesn't want her to have done it, Liz thought. "A lot of the evidence is circumstantial," she said, mainly because she had heard it said on the telly.

"It's just such a nightmare. I thought if the police had the person that did it, then maybe we could start to grieve. Her mum and dad are arriving from France tonight."

Liz wished with all her heart that she had told Bernie she wouldn't go and see Alfie. This was not the time to be interrogating the man.

"I saw your parents downstairs."

Alfie shuffled his feet. "Yeah, I didn't want them to come, but Howie thought they should be here. Dad didn't even like Viola that much."

"And your step-mum?" Liz asked. According to Viola's financial records, she had been working for Newfellow House long before Alfie and her were an item. But as Alfie might not know that, Liz wanted to tread carefully.

"She introduced us. I know it's tradition to not get on with your step-mum, but Rickey's all right. She's certainly a lot more fun than dad."

"And she always has a lot of schemes, isn't that right?"

For the first time, he looked a little evasive. "I guess so."

"I hope you don't take offence at this, Alfie, but I know you had a bit of history with the police where finances were concerned."

Alfie sniffed. "It seemed like such a big deal at the time. Truth is, I was out of my depth. I got involved in these investment schemes, and I promise I thought they were legal. I didn't realise how much trouble we were in until the investments started to fail. Thankfully my dad bailed us all out of it."

This wasn't quite what Liz had expected. The police had painted Alfie as a calculating con artist, but he didn't seem to have the financial wit to con anyone. Could he be covering for other people?

"And was it... did you step-mum get you involved in these schemes?"

"She introduced me to them all. But it was me that made the mistakes, so it was right that I owned up to it all."

Now Liz was sure that Alfie with his influencer lifestyle and fancy clothes had nowhere near the brains to pull off even the smallest con.

"We know that Viola had money coming in from somewhere. Was she involved in some of these investments?"

"Only a little. Sometimes she would help out Rickey by introducing some of her friends who might be looking for investors, that sort of thing."

"What about life coaching?"

"That's all Rickey's side of things. I don't get involved in it. Sometimes she'll ask me to post a video or something to

247

advertise it, but I'm sort of like the face of the business rather than running any of it. I just get to do the fun stuff."

Could anyone be that naïve? Liz almost wanted to shout at Alfie for allowing himself to be the fall guy for all of this. But that wasn't her place, and it wouldn't help the investigation if she got his back up.

"What were your plans after the wedding? Was Viola going to come into the business full time?"

Alfie was beginning to look annoyed. "No. Like I told you, she was barely involved in the first place. In fact, she was planning to step away from it all. We wanted a fresh start, you know?"

Oh dear, Liz thought. There was no sign from Viola's accounts that she was stepping away from the scams. If anything, she had been more involved than ever at the time of her death.

"Thank you for your help, Alfie," Liz said.

The man nodded and she showed herself out. Liz couldn't help feeling that instead of a suspect, she had just discovered another victim.

Chapter 35: Bernie

Bernie found Mary in reception chatting with Walker.

"Just who I wanted to see," Bernie said, glaring at the policeman. "Why didn't you tell us you were going to arrest Nora?"

Walker blinked. "I didn't realise that the entire workforce of Police Scotland had to look for approval from Bernadette Paterson."

"No need to get shirty," Bernie replied. "Maybe if you had let me know first I could have saved you from making a terrible mistake."

"A mistake? Do you have some evidence that proves Nora couldn't have done it?"

"Not yet."

"Then what makes you think she is innocent?"

"Well, for one thing, she had sense enough to employ the WWC to clear her name, so she can't be stupid enough to commit murder."

Walker groaned. "You're working for Nora Hammond now? I thought you were joking when you said that," he said to Mary.

"Why would I joke about that?" Mary pouted.

"I don't know. I don't always understand your jokes. I still don't get the one about Big Bird, the King of Monaco and a Dalek."

"It's too intellectual for you," Mary said.

Bernie tutted. She wasn't paying the woman to stand around and flirt. "Come on, Mary, we've got real work to be getting on with. When you're in the private investigation business, you don't get to just stand around eating biscuits."

"It's the shortbread from the room," Walker said, wiping the crumbs from his jumper. "It's not half bad."

"Refined sugar and saturated fat are not my ideas of 'not half bad'." Bernie replied, but Walker had already pulled out his phone and was speaking to some other police officer on it, judging by the regular use of the word 'Sir'.

While Walker was away, Bernie grabbed Mary's arm.

"I've just seen Liz. She had a meeting with Alfie."

"God, that must have been awful. Is she okay?"

Bernie scowled at her. "I didn't ask. Anyway, we've found a connection to Alfie's stepmother. It turns out she's one of the founders of this Newfellow House business. I don't understand half of what Liz says about investments and bank accounts, but it seems like Viola was working for Alfie's stepmother to get new recruits into the business, then rip them off somehow."

"How does that connect to Viola's murder?"

250

"I'm not sure yet."

Mary clicked her tongue. "If anything, it just backs up the case for Nora being involved. If what Viola was involved in was so dodgy, there was no chance of her getting her money back. Maybe we're wrong and Nora did kill her."

"I can see Nora murdering someone, she is ruthless, ambitious and cold. But I just don't think there was enough reason here. To smother someone, you've got to be really angry with them, don't you? I just can't see it."

Bernie could tell Mary wasn't convinced. She checked her watch. The afternoon was creeping onward and soon they would be out of time. She had to get tough.

"Right, I'm off."

"Where are you going?" Mary asked.

"To the bar."

"Sounds good. Can I come?"

"No. I'm not going for a drink. I'm going to speak to Alfie's parents. I saw them heading that way a minute ago. I just had to wait until your friendly Bobby left so that he didn't see me go over to them. He'd only accuse me of impeding an investigation or something."

Leaving Mary in Reception, Bernie strode over to her destination. The bar was wood panelled in a way that is meant to suggest elegance but just ends up looking sort of grimy. Seated in one of the bay windows were Alfie's father and

251

stepmother.

Bernie ordered herself a gin and slim-line tonic from the bar – an allowable expense for the tax man – and made her way over to them.

"Hello, I'm Bernie Paterson. I'm a private investigator."

Both Callford and his wife stiffened.

"I was also on the hen-do with Viola," Bernie said, hoping that might make them a little more talkative.

"Terrible business," Iain Callford said, then looked down at his phone where he seemed to be taking an interest in the football results.

"We were very fond of Viola," Riccarda said. "It is all too sad." She still had a strong Italian accent and was very beautiful in that European sophisticated way that always made Bernie feel like she should be in a field somewhere digging up tatties.

"As I understand it, you met her before Alfie did."

Riccarda, or Rickey as she was known, gave Bernie a piercing look. "Yes."

"You were in business together."

Now the woman looked to her husband to rescue her, but he was still engrossed in his phone. "She never worked for me."

"Not in an official capacity, but –"

"I'm not sure why you are asking me this."

Bernie stood her ground. "We are trying to find out why she was killed."

"The police have already arrested someone."

"Yes, but she hasn't been charged yet," Bernie replied, hoping that it was still true. "The police believe that money might have been a motive. And Nora claims that Viola owed her money."

Rickey shrugged. "That is nothing to do with me."

"But you were one of the directors of Newfellow House, is that right?"

"That company is no longer trading."

Bernie checked the notes that Liz had sent her. "But you have set up several companies since, all in the same area, haven't you?"

"Not at all. My present company is nothing to do with Newfellow House."

"This would be Life Upgrade Ltd. From what we can tell, Viola was finding contacts for you and funnelling money through this company. These investors didn't seem to get much money flowing back in the opposite direction."

"You have entirely the wrong impression of what we do. We provide a holistic approach. Finance is such a small part of what we offer. It is truly life coaching, each element of your life must be in harmony in order to succeed. Can I give you some leaflets?"

"No. What about the police case? The one where you had to bail Alfie's company out of trouble?"

The smile dropped from Rickey's face. "That was a previous company. It is no longer trading."

"But that's the old trick, isn't it? Fold the company then set up the same thing with a different name? There's a chippy down the road from me that keeps doing the same thing."

If the Italian woman's expression could kill, Bernie would be six feet under.

"You are a very rude woman."

"Yes, I am. It's how I get things done. Now, I want to understand exactly the relationship between you and Viola. Was she working for you before you set her up as a wife for your stepson?"

"That's it. I'm going up to my room. Iain, are you coming?"

"In a few minutes," Iain said. There was little indication he had listened to anything that had just happened.

Without the support of her husband, Rickey flounced out of the room.

There was no invitation to sit down, but Bernie took the seat opposite Iain Callford that his wife had vacated.

"I wonder if I could press you to put your phone away."

"You're a feisty one, aren't you," Mr Callford said with what could only be described as a guffaw. Bernie was fascinated as she had never actually heard one before.

"Feisty?"

"Aye, if you were ten years younger you'd be just my type."

If the man was looking to offend her, then he had chosen the wrong target. When you had spent as long as Bernie had avoiding bottom pinching and general lechery by sleazy old men on a daily basis, one sexist pig barely registered.

"The police were questioning Alfie earlier," Bernie said. "Do you realise that all this dodgy financial dealing puts your son in the frame for Viola's murder?"

Callford looked at her. "The police have already arrested someone else."

"Yes, but they're only going to keep digging. All of this is going to come out at the trial."

"Nonsense," he said, but he didn't sound too sure.

"You don't think that your son might be in a bit of difficulty, then?" She said, sticking to the point of the interview.

"No. Any fool can see that Alfie is broken up over the whole thing."

Bernie waited.

The man sighed. "Do you want me to be honest with you? I had no idea about half the things that Rickey has been getting up to. I thought these little companies she was running were a way for her to have something to do. It's very boring for her, you see. All her family are in Italy, and she's never adapted to the Scottish weather. So when she got involved in these schemes, I didn't think too much about them. Then the police got involved and started to bandy about the word 'fraud'. Alfie took the fall for that one, by the way."

Callford took a gulp of his wine. Bernie was amazed at how quickly he had gone from jovial eccentric rich stereotype to something else entirely.

"I told Rickey then, no more of the fraud stuff. When she set up this life coaching thing, I thought it was some airy-fairy crap. It wasn't until recently that I realised it was the same scam, just wrapped up in a different way."

"Did you know Viola was involved?"

"Not really. I knew that Rickey had met her through work, but I didn't realise that Viola was part of the Life Upgrade nonsense. You're sure she was?"

"Definitely. It's all there in the bank records."

"Then it might be that someone killed her because she was a con artist, just like my wife. But it wasn't Alfie. He would have no need to. I would always bail him out of any trouble, just like I have done before. And just like I will do now, just as soon as I shut down all this life coaching stuff."

"What will Rickey say about that?"

"It won't matter. We'll be divorced in a few months."

"Where were you on the night Viola was killed?"

Callford grinned. "Paris. I just flew back this morning. Why?"

Bernie stood up to go. "Because you seem like just the sort of person that would murder anyone who got in your way."

He tipped his wine glass towards her. "As do you. Good luck with your investigation."

"Thanks," said Bernie, uncomfortably aware that she might have just met her match.

Chapter 36: Walker

Walker was carrying evidence boxes down the stairs of the hotel when he bumped into Mary.

"Moving out, are we?" she asked.

"Back to the station."

"It's sorted then?" Mary said, her tone suggesting she was not impressed. "You've all made up your minds?"

"It is up to the jury to do that," he reminded her. "But our investigations are still ongoing for the moment at least."

"You're such a pedant when you're in uniform," Mary complained.

He gave her a wink. "I thought you liked me in uniform."

She didn't rise to the bait. "Have you had a chance to look into all this Newfellow House stuff? I know that it gives Nora a motive, but there are plenty of others that are in the same position. Every time Liz looks she comes up with someone else that they were swindling."

"Of course we have," Walker said, although he hadn't entirely followed that part of the investigation. He only knew that Nora believed that Viola owed her a lot of money.

"Look, we don't really consider motive," he said, "we're looking at the evidence. You know about Viola's phone, and

258

along with the other physical evidence, it's enough to put Nora before the Procurator Fiscal."

"What other physical evidence?" Mary asked.

Walker sighed. He didn't know why he tried to pretend that he wasn't just going to tell the WWC everything. It would make his life easier if he just gave in. "All right, but this isn't public knowledge, okay? Forensics came back on the pillow. They found traces of nail polish. The same kind that Nora was wearing."

"Just as Bernie… I mean, that doesn't prove anything, does it? Couldn't it have been someone wearing the same colour, or…"

"No. It's a chemical match. It's exactly the same nail polish and we've checked, no one else was wearing it."

Walker could see the tiny frown lines appear between Mary's eyebrows as she tried to think her way around the problem.

"Well, maybe she touched the pillow some other time."

"And I'm sure that's what the defence will argue in court. But you have to agree that it looks suspicious. The only physical evidence on the pillow was Viola's blood and Nora's nail polish."

"I just don't see that it's enough to put her above anyone else. We know that Pru, for example, lost money too, but you haven't arrested her."

"Do you think we should?"

259

"No. Because she… well, she's got some good reasons for not wanting to go to jail for murder right now. But anyway, I'm just saying that there are other possibilities."

"Well, once you have a possibility with an evidentiary link to Viola's death, you let me know," Walker said.

Mary looked annoyed, and he gave her a quick kiss, hoping none of his colleagues were around to see.

"Maybe I'll be able to drive you back to Invergryff tonight," he said.

"Maybe," she said. She had that face that Walker was used to seeing in a relationship. The 'I'm going to be annoyed with you for a good while yet' face. Not for the first time, he wondered how they were going to navigate this whole police officer dating private detective thing.

"Right, I'll see you later then."

"You will," Mary said, her smile more genuine this time.

After Mary left, Walker got on the phone to Macleod.

"I've been thinking about this pillowcase," he said once he had been put through to the DI. "Have we looked at any other trace evidence on it?"

"I don't think there was anything significant, but I can have the techs double-check. What are you worried about?"

"Our case hinges on quite a small amount of physical evidence. I'd like to know if there was anything on the pillowcase that

260

might indicate a different suspect."

"Or anything that could confirm that Nora Hammond is the killer. All right, we'll take another look and I'll get back to you. But remember, the custody clock is ticking."

Walker didn't need reminding. In less than a day, they would have to either charge Nora or let her go, no matter what evidence he did or did not discover.

He checked his watch. It was nearly five, but there was no chance of knocking off work any time soon. Walker had hoped that Mary might have grabbed a takeaway with him somewhere, but that didn't seem likely. He decided to get a sandwich from the hotel bar. He had already eaten all the shortbread in his room, so there wasn't much of an alternative.

Chapter 37: Mary

"Thank god I've found you," Liz said when she turned up at Mary's hotel room after dinner. "Why didn't you answer your phone?"

"I was on a video call with my mum and the kids," Mary explained. "My mum's had to take them as Matt's working away for a few days. She was asking where I kept the school uniforms. I had to explain that they were all piled up in the kitchen. Then she asked me where the iron was, and I don't think she was impressed by my answer."

"Which was?"

"I don't have one," Mary admitted.

"I mean, that's asking for a comment, but I'll leave it," Liz said. "Look, I've found something online and you're never going to believe it."

Liz took out her phone and let Mary see the screen. It was an event listing for a seminar titled 'Upgrade your Goals' with the picture of a shiny-faced young man grinning widely.

"What am I looking at?"

"This guy, Patrick something-or-other, he's giving an introduction to the 'philosophy' of an organisation called Life Upgrade. Life Upgrade are only a couple of company name changes away from Newfellow House and Rickey Callford is one of the directors."

Mary tried to get her head around this. "You mean, this is the same kind of con as Newfellow House? They're still at it?"

"Exactly. And the thing is, this seminar is on tonight, over in Stirling. That's only an hour and a half away. I reckon we've got to get over there."

Mary felt like he was missing something. "But we're in Aviemore. Under house arrest. I mean, I know the police said they couldn't make us stay, but they'll definitely be asking questions if we disappear off all of a sudden."

Liz's mouth turned down at the corners. "Come on Mary, I'm dying to get a break from this place. We can just sneak out."

Mary's inner goodie two shoes was vying with her desire to get out of the hotel. "Are you sure we should?"

"Why not? Technically they can't keep us here, but if we're clever they won't even realise we're gone. If we don't tell them we're leaving then they'll never know and we can just sneak back in later on."

"What does Bernie think about all this?"

Liz laughed. "Whose idea do you think it was? She would have come with us, but she said she doesn't want to let the other suspects out of her sight. I think she's still a bit sore that Viola's murder happened right under our noses."

"All right then," Mary said, starting to get excited about the idea. "How are we going to get through to Stirling?"

"We will need transportation. And something a bit more subtle than a bloody tank this time."

"Ooh, we can be like Thelma and Louise," Mary said, then added, "without the cliff bit."

"Definitely without the cliff. Your Sergeant Walker has a car, doesn't he?"

"Yes. But I'm not sure he'll be too happy about taking us."

"He doesn't have to. Just get him to add me on the insurance for a night and I'll drive us."

"Um…"

"Come on, I'm sure you can sweet talk him into it."

Mary frowned. It seemed like her relationship with Walker was fast becoming an often used resource for the other members of the WWC. She wasn't sure she liked the trend.

Ten minutes later, she was in the back of the car with Liz while Walker drove them to Stirling.

"I can't believe I'm doing this," he said, not for the first time.

"You could have let me take the car," Liz said, rubbing her swollen ankles.

"That's a whole world of trouble I would rather avoid, thank you very much."

Mary kept quiet. It had taken all of her persuasive skills, plus the promise to watch the next three football matches with him, to get Walker to let them out in the first place.

"Have you got any antacids?" Liz asked.

"No."

"Shame," Liz said, placing her hand on her bump. "This baby feels like it's trying to claw its way out through my throat."

Mary stifled a laugh when she saw Walker's horrified expression.

"They can't do that, you know," she told him.

"I know. But I'll never get that image out of my head, thank you very much. Can I put the radio on? I like to listen to rock music when I drive."

"Ugh, what is it with white men and soft rock," Liz said.

Mary winced. Pregnancy was making her friend more grumpy than usual.

"Fine. No radio."

There was silence for a few minutes.

"Can't you put the flashing lights on?" Liz asked.

Mary made shushing motions at her friend while Walker's back stiffened.

"He's not allowed to do that," Mary said in a low tone.

"Have you asked him before?"

Walker let out a laugh from the front seat. "Every bloody time." Then he turned the radio onto Classic Rock.

Chapter 38: Liz

"We should split up," Liz said as they got out of the car in Stirling. "We'll have more chance to find out something if we talk to people separately. And it means if they work out that one of us isn't interested in their sales pitch the other one can keep pretending.

"Maybe I'll want to sign up," Mary said. "I mean, we only know of two people who have been bankrupted by the scheme. I might end up as an influencer and people can send me free clothes."

"I'm not sure those people shop at the same places you do," Liz said to Mary. Her friend had toned down her peculiar sense of personal style this evening, but she was still wearing her favourite Doc Martens and a badge on her coat that send 'Love Books, Hate People'."

"Oi," Walker called, rolling down the window. "Are you sure I shouldn't come in?"

Liz shook her head. "Everything about you screams copper. You might spook them. Much better if we go in ourselves."

She took Mary by the arm before Walker had a chance to say anything else, and marched into the hotel.

A sign in Reception pointed them towards the ballroom, a grand name for a large room with eighties decor that had never seen a ball. When they walked in they were greeted by several posters of the speaker, Patrick Errol and his long list of accomplishments which seemed to be building a 'property empire' and appearing on daytime TV around five years ago.

Liz knew that this man was merely the face of the newest incarnation of Newfellow House, now called Life Upgrade. She wondered if Errol knew just how dodgy the company was, and if he even cared.

"Would you like a glass of fizz?" A young South Asian woman with large teeth and a hungry expression handed them two glasses.

Liz put hers back on the tray. "Sorry, I can't."

The woman noticed her bump. "There's orange juice too."

"Don't worry about it." Liz pretended not to notice that Mary was quite cheerily downing her glass of wine. "This is the first time we've been to one of these things."

"Oh, that's great, you're in for a treat. Patrick is, like, so inspiring. Before I started the programme I was three stone heavier!"

That explained the wolfish smile.

"I didn't realise it was a weight loss thing."

"No, not at all. It's a holistic lifestyle programme. I was, like, manifesting the weight loss. And then I spent a year in the gym and eating a limited calorie diet and here I am!"

"Amazing," Mary said, with more sincerity than Liz would

have managed.

With a quick nod at her friend, Mary moved away and started to walk around the room. The idea was to mingle with the other attendees and find out what they knew about the newly reinvented Newfellow House organisation. Although, Liz noted, Mary appeared to be too shy to actually go up and speak to anyone, so she wasn't sure how that would work.

"Hello," Liz said to a couple in their fifties who were wearing matching chinos. "Have you been to one of these before?"

"Oh yes," the wife said, her cheeks pink from the wine. "We were part of the first course intake in London last year. We're looking for people to invest in our property empire. We want to share our success with others."

Liz didn't like how close they were standing to her. "Property empire? That sounds impressive."

"We've got two in the pipeline right now," the man said. Liz suspected he had had a hair transplant as he had an odd recently planted forest situation going on across his forehead.

"Oh that's great," Liz replied, feeling her smile start to sag. "How many have you done already?"

The woman's lips curled downwards. "Well, just those two, and our own home, which we doubled in value. With the right investment, we'll be looking at six properties a year."

"Right. Well, I hope you find it," Liz said, moving away towards the seats that had been set out for the talk. The sad thing was, she thought, that a short course in accountancy or business would give these people so many more skills than all these get rich quick courses.

A few minutes later, someone called out that people should take their seats and then the speaker appeared on stage in a rather shiny royal blue suit.

Liz's first thought was that the man was smiling a little too much. It reminded her of when Bernie's cat Witch was trying to pinch her tuna sandwich.

The shiny suit announced himself as Patrick Errol. He had an accent that suggested somewhere around the Midlands and eyebrows that were so perfectly shaped that Liz was wondering if she should ask for the name of his salon.

The audience was an odd mix. Liz was one of the older people there. There were a few couples, whispering to one another while looking at their phones. Lots of single men whose attire suggested they would be staying single for the foreseeable future. And lots of women in jeans with blazers on top. Liz couldn't decide if she was over or under dressed, but she felt like she didn't quite fit in. Maybe it was the air of desperation that the others were emanating that set her apart.

The whispering stopped as Errol took to the stage and started up his presentation. There was a screen behind him showing the branding for Life Upgrade Ltd. This, Liz knew, was the latest incarnation of what had at one time been called Newfellow House.

The speech was carefully constructed. It reminded Liz of when you saw politicians on the TV. The speaker managed to

270

fill the time with plenty of fancy words, but without very many hard facts. There were several mentions of 'manifesting' which seemed to be a thing where you asked for lots of money and it would magically present itself. Liz wondered if she could manifest some heartburn tablets. She shouldn't have eaten so much shortbread. Or maybe it was the speech that was giving her chest pains.

"And what can coaching do for you? Let's look at one of our case studies, shall we?"

To Liz's surprise, a picture of Alfie Callford appeared on the screen.

"Here's Alfie, one of our earlier Peer Partners. Alfie came to us without any idea what he wanted to do, but he had ambition in spades. And look at him now! Nearly a million followers across all his social media platforms and he's about to start his own coaching series!

There was polite applause to this, which the man on stage received as if it was rampant cheers. Liz was unimpressed. The speaker had made no mention of the fact that before his 'manifesting' had begun Alfie had been born into a family that owned a multimillion pound hotel chain.

Several more examples followed. Liz made a note of them all to check out later. There were two happy, Botox-faced women, standing in front of ugly modern rendered houses, and an older man driving a convertible along a beach road who had retired at fifty. And, of course, the obligatory smiling black guy, waving at the audience in front of a collage of his property empire. Liz wondered if he was a stock photo, given that she and the skinny woman who handed out glasses of wine were the only people of colour there that evening.

Everything about the seminar screamed 'scam', yet no one seemed to be running for the hills. In fact, when the talk was over there was a rush to the front as everyone wanted to be the first to speak to Errol personally.

Liz looked over at Mary, who, behind the cover of her leaflet, mimed puking. Liz hid a smile. At least her friend wasn't fooled.

She sat still in her seat and thought about what she had learned. What had all of this to do with Viola's death? Liz was sure there was a connection. Life Upgrade or Newfellow House, whatever it was called, it wasn't just a financial scam. They were selling people dreams, giving them hope of a wonderful life that they never had a chance of attaining. That was the sort of thing that someone would kill for. Had that been Nora's motive? From what they had learned, the woman the police had arrested was looking more likely to be the killer than ever. Unless they could find another connection to someone else at the cottage. Tired, with sore feet and heartburn stinging her chest, Liz made her way over to Mary.

The woman had found – or been found by – one of the earnest female attendees.

"It all started with some candles, if you can imagine?"

"Is that right?" Mary had a glazed expression.

"Yes. I learned how to make my own online shop. It didn't

take long at all to recoup the initial outlay for equipment and so on. And then I went to franchising, which is the key to passive income, as you'll know."

"Of course."

"And I'm always looking for new investors. Your brand new life can start today! Can I give you my number?"

"Oh, um…"

Liz touched Mary on the arm. "Time for us to head off," she said firmly. Mary gave her a look like she had been saved from the deck of the Titanic.

The other woman made a sour face, then turned to find someone else to talk to. Mary and Liz watched her go. For a few seconds neither said a word.

"Wow," Liz managed.

"Double wow," Mary said. "You know, I didn't really get it when you said this place was like a cult, but now I see it."

"Yeah, let's head back to the hotel," Liz said, following Mary out of the building. "I don't know, all this talk about a new life. I'd just settle for one hour when my feet don't hurt and my bladder doesn't need emptied."

"That's the dream," Mary replied.

Chapter 39: Bernie

Bernie walked around the hotel, looking for something to occupy her while Liz and Mary were at the seminar. She could have gone with them, of course, but she didn't like to leave the hotel full of suspects unguarded.

Of course, there was a whole division of police officers there, but as far as Bernie was concerned, they wouldn't be able to find their arses with their truncheons.

Still, at least she could get her steps in. She checked her fitness watch. Nearly twelve thousand for the day. The lack of internet at the cottage had meant that her unbroken streak of seven hundred odd days had been, well, broken. It had irritated her, but not as much as Viola's murder had.

She walked outside the hotel to get some fresh air. It was a clear night, still with an edge of chill that the snow had left, but dark and beautiful with the stars shining bright overhead. There was something to be said, she admitted grudgingly, for being outside of her usual urban environment.

A movement from a few meters away drew her eye. Someone had stepped out of the bar onto a small terrace and was staring at their phone.

"Checking if you've gained any new members tonight?" Bernie said, appearing at the woman's shoulder.

Rickey Callford put her phone back into her pocket.

"Whatever are you talking about?"

"The seminar in Stirling. It must be finishing up around now. I wonder if your man in the cheap suit did a good job peddling your fool's gold."

Mrs Callford glowered at her from impeccably shaped eyebrows. "I do not understand why you feel you can talk to me like this."

"Because you're a criminal and my job is to catch criminals. Sadly, you're the sort of criminal who gets everyone else to do their dirty work."

"If you continue with these allegations –"

"What? You won't do a thing," Bernie said. "The last thing you want is news of your schemes becoming public."

"I'm going to my room."

"Fine. But you better watch your back."

The woman looked around as if she expected someone to save her, but there was no one else around.

"Are you threatening me?"

Bernie nodded. "Certainly."

"Outrageous!"

"Not really. Now, my friends tell me that I'm old-fashioned in the way I do things," Bernie said with a shrug. "I disagree. I don't think it's old-fashioned to believe in right and wrong.

And you've known for a long time that what you were doing was wrong. Now your stepson's heart is broken. His future wife is dead. I think you have to take some of the blame for that."

"I didn't kill her."

"Yes, you did, the minute you signed her up to this business. Did you really think you would get away with it forever?"

Mrs Callford straightened her back. "You know nothing about me. Where I grew up in Napoli we had to fight for every single thing we had. I'm not going to let you or your silly Scottish police force take that away."

Bernie laughed. "This isn't *The Godfather*. Honestly, your deprived childhood in Napoli? You're on your third rich husband since then. You can hardly plead poverty."

"I don't need to justify myself to you."

"No, but when this all comes out in the papers, you will need to justify yourself to the police. And to all the people you've swindled."

Pushed to her limit, Rickey Callford turned on her heel and strode back into the hotel. Bernie allowed herself a tiny smile. It wouldn't make any difference to the investigation, of course, if she got the Callfords rattled. But it did make her feel better to see the smug expression wiped from the stupid woman's face.

Bernie stifled a yawn just as a car pulled up outside the hotel. She ran to meet Liz and Mary.

"I'm off to bed," Walker said, rather curtly when Bernie reached the car. "If you need a taxi again tonight, I'm sure the hotel can hook you up."

The man strode off towards his room.

"He's always like this if he doesn't get his eight hours," Mary said, with an indulgent smile.

"Come upstairs and tell me all about the seminar," Bernie said.

Liz folded her arms across her chest. "Mary can tell you. I'm off to bed. If I don't take my weight off my feet they'll be like watermelons tomorrow."

Bernie turned to Mary who couldn't think of an excuse quickly enough.

"Sure. Can we order room service?"

"No. But I'll make you a tea."

By the time Bernie had made the tea, Mary had already eaten a packet of shortbread.

"You know you won't metabolise those calories while you're sleeping," Bernie told her.

"Tell someone who cares," Mary said popping another biscuit into her mouth. In truth, Bernie felt a little proud. Last year little mousey Mary Plunkett would never have stood up for herself like that.

"So what happened at this seminar?" Bernie asked, handing over the cup of tea.

277

Mary gave her a brief summary of the night and the nonsense that the speaker was spouting. Bernie was glad she hadn't gone. She wouldn't have been able to sit there in silence while the man on the stage told his lies.

"And you don't think there was anything relevant to our investigation?"

"Not exactly. It was more the general air of desperation. Honestly, it's a wonder none of them were murdered before now. And there was one other thing, but it might be nothing."

"What was that?"

"Liz mentioned that Tryss was into all this modern home-maker stuff. You know, pickling her own produce, organic farming, make do and mend. She told us herself she had a little farm shop, do you remember?"

Bernie nodded.

"Well, one of the things Tryss was interested in was candle making. And when I was talking to one of the women at the seminar, that was how she got started. They encourage all these 'side hustles', you see, and one of the popular ones is candle making."

"That doesn't prove much, does it?"

"No. But Liz is going to take another look at Tryss's accounts. See if she can find any connection there."

"Quiet wee Trystesse," Bernie mused. "Could she be the killer? Viola was her cousin."

"The thing is," Mary added, "I always thought it was a bit weird that Tryss was on the hen-do in the first place. She was so clearly miserable. I don't like to think of her as a murderer, but when you look at it logically…"

Bernie nodded. "It makes sense. Let's see what Liz comes up with tomorrow."

Mary pulled out her phone. "Man, it's after midnight. I better get to bed."

"And tomorrow we're going to catch a killer," Bernie said.

Mary gave her a tired smile. "I hope so."

Chapter 40: Walker

Walker woke up to his alarm on Tuesday morning with a weird sense of dislocation. It was partly because Mary had changed his alarm sound to the noise the Tardis made when it landed, but also because he was still in Aviemore. One of those things would be rectified today at least, because he had no idea how to fix the alarm.

He made his way into the incident room, which was looking very bare. A few constables were removing the last of the computer equipment.

Sergeant Hughson handed him a forensic report. "The boss said you asked for this. The lab took another look at the trace evidence. They found an oily substance on the pillow. Some sort of moisturizer type stuff. Traces of an emollient which has a high glycerine base, whatever that means. We know that Nora was a beautician, so we're hoping to match it up with one of her lotions and potions."

"Right," Walker said. He was pleased that they had found evidence that might make the case against Nora Hammond stronger, but he knew that Mary wouldn't be too happy about it.

"You look tired, Walker," Macleod said, walking past with a bacon roll in one hand.

"I had to drive back from Stirling last night. Didn't get to bed until well after midnight."

"Stirling? What were you doing in Stirling?"

Walker handed him one of the flyers from the seminar. "Mary persuaded me to take her to this. The guy who gave the talk isn't anyone we know, but the company that runs it is the same one that Viola was working for. The same one that Alfie's stepmother runs."

Macleod's brow creased. "And why is that relevant?"

"It's all connected, sir. Viola was only on the fringes of the organisation. She introduced people to those higher up the tree. They get them to start with small investments at first, then larger ones, until they are so committed that they can't see a way out."

"You make it sound like a cult."

"It works the same way. This whole 'life coaching' thing is just an attempt to make it look legitimate."

"All right, you've convinced me that we need to flag this up to the fraud department. But I don't see how it's relevant to our murder case."

Walker paused. He knew he was largely working on conjecture now. "Well, it means that there are a lot more people with a motive to kill Viola than we initially thought."

Macleod rubbed his chin. "But not many with the opportunity to kill her. We know that the killer was one of the women in the house with her that night."

"And the physical evidence points towards Nora. I know. But

281

I think there's still a good deal of reasonable doubt that one of the others could have done it. I'd like you to keep the investigation open just a little longer so I can check them out."

"This wouldn't have anything to do with your friends and their detective agency?"

There was little point in denying it. "They think there's a case that someone else might be involved. And... well, it seems that Nora has engaged them to clear her name."

Macleod then said some words that were quite surprising for a man of the Free Church. Once he had calmed down he said: "If they screw up this investigation, I will singlehanded kick their arses back to the Central Belt."

"I understand. The thing is, we might as well have them on our side rather than working against us. We've still got a few more hours before we need to charge Nora. I'm only asking you to hold off on taking the case to the Procurator Fiscal until the WWC have done their thing."

"And what exactly is 'their thing'?"

"I don't know, but it seems to work out a surprising amount of the time."

For a minute, Walker thought the DI was going to tell him to get lost, then Macleod let out a long sigh.

"You know, Walker, if you stick your neck out on this one and it all goes wrong, I won't be able to protect you from the consequences?"

"Yes sir."

"Then tell your friends to do their stuff. And do it in the next three hours."

Chapter 41: Mary

Mary struggled to get up on Tuesday. It had been late by the time she'd gone to sleep and she had dreamed of men with fixed grins trying to sell her candles.

Unable to face Bernie without some caffeine in her system, she went down to the restaurant to grab some breakfast. Liz was already there.

"Mind if I sit down?" Mary said, bringing over a plate full of fried breakfast.

"Sure."

"Something wrong?" Mary pointed at the yoghurt and single banana that Liz had picked out to eat.

"Yeah, I was up half the night with heartburn," Liz said, rubbing her bump. "I think it's time to lay off the breakfast buffets."

Mary speared a sausage with her fork. "Pregnancy sucks big time. But it's worth it in the end."

"Oh, I know. The product is good but the process leaves a lot to be desired. What did you think of the seminar last night?"

"I think I understand things a little better," Mary said once she had finished chewing. "When you were talking about investments and things, I didn't quite get it. But now I do. They were selling hope. Those people last night, they were so desperate to be successful – whatever the hell that means – that they couldn't see the wood for the trees. And those are the sort of people that Viola was preying on. She was… well, not the sort of person I thought she was."

"No," Liz said, and they were both quiet for a minute.

Hailey walked into the room. For a moment, she looked like she would pretend she hadn't noticed them, but then she made her way over to the table.

"I'm getting the lunchtime train back home today," Hailey told them. "I wish I could say it's been nice knowing you guys but, well, it's been like something out of a horror film."

"It's a shame it all ended so badly," Mary said.

"Yeah. I don't think I'll be volunteering to be a bridesmaid again for a while." Hailey hands twisted together. "Could you… could you tell Bernie I'm sorry I punched her? I don't think I was quite myself."

"Oh, don't worry about it," Liz said. "Bernie's already over it. It's not the first time someone has decked her one. I don't even think it's the first time this month."

"Good," Hailey said, looking relieved.

Something struck Mary that she had been meaning to ask the woman. "Do you know why Tryss told us that thing about you and Viola arguing about a prenup?"

Hailey shrugged. "No. Tryss must have got the wrong end of the stick about it. I told you before, I wanted to stay out of all

Viola's legal troubles. The less I knew the better. And the same went for Tryss."

"For Tryss?"

"Yeah, she wanted me to give her some legal advice about something too. Honestly, if you had a friend who was a doctor you wouldn't ask them to examine your colon, but for some reason as soon as you practice law everyone wants free advice."

"What did Tryss want to know?"

"No idea, but she was all agitated about it. Shame she's already gone home or you could ask her yourself."

Liz gave Mary a significant look. "Tryss has gone home?"

"She didn't even wait for breakfast. She said the lambs needed her." Hailey rolled her eyes at that. "Anyway, I'm off now. Don't take this the wrong way, but I hope we never see each other again."

"Ouch," Mary said, once the woman had left. "I don't think we made a friend there."

"No, but wasn't it interesting what she said about Tryss."

Mary nodded. She popped a bit of bacon into her mouth and was disappointed to learn it had gone cold.

Liz was still talking. "Why would Tryss tell us that the chat with Hailey had been about a prenup when she knew fine well it was about Newfellow House? It doesn't make sense."

"Unless the truth would somehow put pressure on Tryss

286

herself?" Mary suggested.

"All right. Let's go up to my room. I want to take a look at some things on my laptop."

Mary only had time to grab a singular Danish pastry as they left the restaurant and went upstairs.

"Right," Liz said when she had sat down on the bed and started up her laptop. "I'm going to need to concentrate, so sit still and don't say a word."

Silence was not Mary's strongpoint. In fact, she had often been told off in school for talking during class. She was the sort of person that got the giggles at funerals. It took every ounce of her being to stay quiet while Liz worked on her laptop.

Eventually, the other woman stopped.

"Got it," Liz hissed.

"Really."

"Yep. I didn't see it at first, because her personal accounts all looked fine. But when I looked into the business accounts for the croft I realised that she's in all kinds of trouble."

"You think she was another investor in Newfellow House?"

Liz nodded. "The bank account numbers look right. Of course, it's going to be hard to prove given that so much of Newfellow's finances is tangled up and hidden."

"And the police will want physical evidence, but the only thing found in Viola's room to connect anyone to her death was the nail polish on the pillow."

"We still haven't explained that, have we," Mary said.

"No. But I can't shake off this feeling that Tryss might be the one. We know that Viola was about to cause her to lose everything. It gives her a motive. And there's no one to back her up like Pru and Nora do for each other."

"But here's the problem. She's such a little mousy thing. I mean, the idea that Tryss would kill anyone is ludicrous," Mary said.

"Why do I feel like there's a 'but' coming?" Liz asked.

"But she does have the most to lose. I mean, her whole identity is this farmer's wife, crofter type. If someone threatened that…"

Liz nodded. "Doesn't seem quite so ludicrous now, does it?"

"No, it doesn't. You're sure she's in that much trouble?"

"She can't make the mortgage payments. It's only a matter of time before the bank takes the farm. Do you think she would kill her cousin to keep it?"

Mary inclined her head slightly in assent. "Yes, I do."

"Then how the hell are we going to prove it?"

"I don't know. But we're going to have to do something nasty and probably illegal."

"I'll get Bernie then."

Ten minutes later their illustrious leader had joined them, sporting a lycra outfit that left little to the imagination.

"What are you wearing?" Liz asked.

"I found the hotel gym today," Bernie replied. "They've got a cross-trainer. You can tell I'm out of shape, my heart rate was sky high."

She started doing a weird series of lunges in the hotel room which was barely big enough for three people let alone one middle-aged athlete.

"Knock it off, Berns," Liz said. "You're making me nauseous."

"Everything makes you nauseous right now," Bernie said.

"Yes, but your sweaty thighs are definitely not helping. Besides, we've got something important to tell you."

Liz caught Bernie up on the latest results of her financial investigations into Trystesse's business accounts while Mary surreptitiously tried to brush the Danish crumbs from her top.

The sound of the Enterprise D Class going into Warp Speed came out of her phone.

"Hang on, Walker's ringing."

"Don't tell him we've solved the case yet," Bernie urged her.

"I won't because we haven't," Mary said, then she clicked the answer button.

"Hi, I'm with Bernie and Liz," she said before he could speak.

"Thanks for the warning. Actually, I'm glad they're with you. I might just have something for you, but as usual you can't tell –"

"I know, I know, it's confidential."

"Right. I just got the techs to take a look at the ingredients of an oily substance that was found on Viola's pillow. The lab have checked and it turns out that it's not a match for any of Nora's toiletries. But we have worked out what it is. It's an intensive, glycerine based moisturizer that is used for hand cream."

"Hand cream?"

Bernie clapped her hands together. "Tryss uses hand cream. The Norwegian formula stuff."

"Bernie says that Trystesse uses Norwegian formula hand cream," Mary told Walker.

He went silent for a second. "You might just be on to something here. That sounds like the stuff on the pillow."

Bernie was hopping from one foot to the other in excitement.

"Can I call you back in a minute," Mary said, pressing the end call button and putting down her phone.

"We've got her," Bernie said, "that's the physical evidence to connect her to the crime."

"There's still Nora's nail polish on the pillow. We haven't

explained that yet."

"We will. Now, what about all this financial stuff with the croft? If you're telling me she was mortgaged up to the hilt, then why didn't we find the connection earlier?" Bernie asked, giving Liz a glare that showed who she thought was to blame.

"All her interactions with Newfellow House were under her maiden name, Trystesse Radford, and she doesn't use it for anything else. Her normal accounts are under Trystesse MacKinnon. There's no financial connection between the two."

"Huh, doesn't seem that tricky."

"Tell me about it once you've got your degree in accountancy," Liz said stiffly.

Sensing a fight on the horizon, Mary turned to Bernie. "Look, we need to see if we're right. And the police aren't going to be interested. They think they've already got their killer. So it's got to be the WWC. I don't suppose you can come up with a way to get her to confess, you know, James Bond villain style."

Bernie sat down on the bed. Mary tried not to think about the sweat that was sinking into the duvet cover.

"We need to set a trap," Bernie said.

"It's a trap," Mary said in a perfect rendition of Admiral Ackbar.

The other two women looked at her.

"Yes," Bernie said slowly, as if Mary had lost her mind. "It is."

"It's a quote from… never mind," Mary said. "Let's just get on with it."

Chapter 42: Liz

Sometimes between Bernie's bluster and Mary's idealism, Liz found she had to be the one to calm her friends down.

"Look," Liz said. "Getting a confession is not like it is on the telly. No one just says 'oho, you caught me, I'm sorry that I did it' in real life, do they?"

"That's why we're going to set a trap," Bernie said. She had already got changed into fresh clothes and was ready to go. "We'll have to get her to confess somehow, then record it and give it to the police."

"Of course we will," Liz rolled her eyes. "And am I going to be the one recording it by any chance?"

"Not at all," Bernie said with a smug little smile. "You're going to be the bait."

Ten minutes later, Liz was in the back of the car with her two friends while Sergeant Walker drove them towards Pitlochry.

Liz could tell that the Sergeant wasn't very happy, even though they had let him drive. He had mentioned 'obstruction' twice, 'interfering in an active investigation' three times and 'bunch of civilians' once before Bernie had given him one of her Looks.

"I don't suppose there's any chance you'll let me do this bit," Walker said when they arrived in Pitlochry. They pulled into a layby that was a quarter of a mile away from the farmhouse.

Bernie tutted at him. "She'll take one look at you and scarper. Look, we've already discussed all this. Liz is going to show her all the financial stuff, then Mary is going to sweet talk her into confessing. Mary will get it all recorded for you."

"Which won't be admissible in court."

"No, but it should be enough to get Nora off and start your lot looking in the right direction. I can't do all the policing for you, you know."

Walker looked like an attack dog that was about to bite until Mary put a calming hand on his arm. Bernie didn't seem to notice.

"Mary will be wearing this earpiece," Bernie continued. "And a tiny camera concealed in this button. It hooks up to an app on this phone. Walker, I thought you might want to hang on to it. It records automatically too."

"Where did you get that?"

"The internet," Bernie said sweetly. "You wouldn't believe what you can buy on there. I ordered it when we got to the hotel and it came by next day delivery."

Walker scowled again.

"Look, we know none of this will be admissible evidence," Mary said to him in the sort of soothing tone Liz had heard her use with her three-year-old. "We just want to make sure an innocent woman isn't convicted for the murder."

That seemed to placate Walker a little. "All right. Now, we're all going to walk over to the croft. From the satellite pictures, there are several barn-type buildings on the West side of the house and I'll make my way to one of them. You go directly to the house."

"It's quite sexy when he gets all bossy, isn't it?" Liz whispered to Mary once they had started walking.

"Shh," the other woman said, but her cheeks were a little pink.

"I'm going to follow a few minutes behind," Bernie said. She seemed a bit annoyed that Walker had started giving orders. "Just shout for me if you need backup."

Thus instructed, Liz and Mary set off together. After a few minutes, Walker veered off to the right and disappeared into some trees. Bernie was somewhere behind them, but they couldn't see her.

The track over to the farmhouse was eerily reminiscent of the one to the cottage, and Liz glanced up at the sky more than once to check that there was no incoming snowfall. When they arrived at their destination they saw a quaint little house with a series of sheds and barns around it. Chickens plucked at worms in the grass and some black-faced sheep looking at them with curiosity from behind a fence.

Liz took a breath and looked over at Mary's whose grim expression mirrored her own. This was not going to be fun. It was one thing to catch a murderer, but quite another when you had found yourself liking them. Still, if what they thought was true, Trystesse deserved to be put away for the rest of her life. If nothing else, it would free an innocent woman who was currently in the police station in Aviemore.

Mary knocked on the door. There was no answer. They looked at one another for a few moments, until Liz realised that there was a bleating sound from around the back.

Her friend led the way as they skirted the perimeter of the house and found Trystesse feeding half a dozen goats of varying sizes and colours.

"What the hell are you doing here?" Tryss asked. She dropped the bucket of animal feed and an opportunistic goat shoved its head into it.

"We've just heard some information about Viola's death and we wanted to tell you before it was on the news," Liz explained. "We were heading past on our way home anyway."

Goats forgotten, Tryss walked over to them. "I didn't realise I had told you where I lived."

"It wasn't hard to work out. There are not that many smallholdings around here," Liz said, not feeling the need to add how easy that sort of information was to come by if you knew your way around a few financial websites.

"Right." Tryss hadn't moved. She seemed in a bit of a daze.

"Is your husband around?" Liz asked.

"No. He's taken the pig to market."

"Like the song," Mary said, delighted.

Tryss frowned. "It's not quite as nice as the song. It's the

296

market and then the abattoir."

"Ah." Mary looked rather less happy.

"That's the reality of farming, you see."

"It can be an expensive business, can't it, running your own croft?"

Tryss rubbed at a patch of mud on her trousers. "Yes. More than you can imagine."

Now was the time to lay their trap. "Oh, I can imagine. I've worked with lots of small businesses in my days as an accountant, and I know how tricky it can be to keep things afloat."

"What are you getting at?"

Liz swallowed. Tryss was too wary to take the bait. "Well, I know that you've re-mortgaged the croft. I'm guessing that was without your husband's knowledge?"

"I wouldn't... how do you know that?"

"You had to do it, didn't you? To pay off the money that you owed to Newfellow House. They invested in your farm, but they wanted you to pay it back at a high interest rate. And you couldn't meet the payments."

Tryss's face had gone pale, but she didn't move a muscle. A small brown bird landed in a bush near them and started to trill out a song.

"Tryss, why don't you tell us what happened with Viola?"

The woman's shoulders dropped and for a moment, Liz thought this was going to be it. Tryss really was going to confess. Then the woman turned on her heels and ran.

"Bloody hell," Liz said, "you'll have to go after her, I'm not exactly Paula Radcliffe at the moment."

Mary nodded and started to jog towards Tryss who was already at the edge of the next field. The woman began climbing over the fence, then stopped as something appeared beside her.

"Stop!" A figure emerged from the ditch like something out of a nightmare. Dripping with mud and slime it was unrecognisable.

Tryss reared backwards and promptly fell over onto her arse. "What the hell?"

"Oh no," Liz said, working out what was happening.

"You're not going anywhere," a wet and slimy Bernie Paterson said, advancing on Tryss.

Meanwhile, Tryss was scuttling backwards and seemed to be heading towards one of the sheds.

"You can't hide from me in there Tryss," Bernie was telling her. "Kill someone while I'm sleeping, would you? You'll pay for this!"

Liz glanced at Mary, who was hanging back, not sure what to do apart from point her button at the mayhem.

"Let Bernie handle it," Liz whispered to her. "She's got

everything under control."

Tryss ducked into one of the sheds, then came back out a few seconds later with something in her hands.

"Oh god," Liz said, the words coming out in a squeak.

"Take one more step and I shoot!" Tryss said as she pointed the gun at Bernie.

Chapter 43: Bernie

The women's hand was shaking so much that Bernie was worried that the gun might go off by accident. She could see out of the corner of her eye that Mary's boyfriend was creeping about in the bushes, about to do something terribly brave.

Sod that, Bernie thought. He'll probably end up getting himself shot and then I'll have to deal with a weepy Mary Plunkett for months.

"Now, Trystesse, you may be a murderer, but you have never once, since I met you, been silly. That gun is very silly. You must put it down right now."

"I must... what? I have a gun, you know."

There was a film of shiny sweat on the woman's brow.

"Yes, I know, and as I said, it is your first mistake in this whole business. Let's go back inside and have a cup of tea."

"A cup of tea? I killed my cousin."

"You did. And I take mine without sugar, as you might imagine." Bernie took a few steps, then, encouraged by the lack of having her brains blasted across the garden, took a few more. She came up next to Tryss, pushed the gun until it was pointing at the floor and then removed it from her limp hands.

"Let's have that cuppa now," Bernie said firmly. She met Walker's eye and placed the gun on the ground. Then she put her arm around Tryss and marched her inside.

Ten minutes later, the members of the WWC were sat around the table with Tryss as she poured them all tea. Bernie had wiped the worst of the slime from her clothes from where she had been hiding in the ditch. Walker was skulking outside somewhere, presumably waiting for the cavalry to turn up.

It was a measure of how odd the situation was that Tryss had provided a plate of biscuits for them, even though they were about to have her jailed for murder. Mary and Liz had already taken two each, even though they were chocolate digestives and that was nearly a quarter of the recommended daily saturated fat. It'd serve them right if Tryss had poisoned them, Bernie thought.

"I should never have trusted her," Tryss was saying as her cup of tea went cold on the table in front of her. "She was always a schemer, even as a child. But I was desperate even before the Newfellow House stuff. The costs of farming have gone up so much recently. The animal feed is twice as much as it was last year, and as for fertilizer…" She trailed off.

"You don't have to speak to us, you know," Mary said in a fit of conscience. "I mean, if you incriminate yourself, it might not look too good at the trial."

Bernie gave Mary's ankles a kick under the table.

"My mum was a Catholic," Tryss said, "I've always been fond of the concept of confession. Besides, I think I rather put my foot in it with the police when I tried to shoot Bernie."

"True," Bernie said with a smile to show her there were no hard feelings. "You were saying about how you went to Viola for help with the farm costs."

"Yes. She said she would find me 'investors'. She even got me making candles, selling stupid beauty products in the farm shop, stuff that I never even got any money for. But it was all part of the lifestyle, wasn't it? Everyone else had had so much success with the programme, I just had to wait for my time. But it never came."

"Did you plan to kill her at the hen-do?" Bernie asked.

"No! I never planned anything. I was going to talk to her, of course, but I still thought that it was all going to work out in the end. Until I heard her talking to Nora and Pru. The Londoners were using words like 'scam' and 'con' and then I realised. I had been conned. And scammed. Up until then I really thought Viola was going to get my money back."

"And what happened that night?" Mary asked gently.

"They were all arguing about money again. As usual, Viola had forgotten I was even in the room. She said that she would pay Nora and Pru back, but she didn't even mention my money. And then I went up to bed."

"But you didn't go to sleep?"

"No. I just got madder and madder. And then I got up to go to the loo and bumped into Viola. She said she had a headache and would I 'be a dear' and get her some aspirin. I mean, the nerve of the woman! But I still didn't do anything.

I brought her the aspirin, then I waited until her light went out. I still didn't realise I was going to do it until I had the pillow over her face."

There was a pause and Bernie looked at her friends, hoping that Mary's recorder had captured that one.

"And afterwards?" Bernie asked.

"It's funny, you would think I would panic, but I didn't. Even when I was still in that bedroom, I knew that there would be plenty of other people to pin it on."

"Like when you took Viola's phone."

"I thought I was quite clever with that one. I took it from beside her bed. I needed to delete any reference to me being part of the Newfellow House stuff. Once I had done that, I just had to wait for my moment. Her phone was the same model as mine, so one time when I was making tea, I asked Nora to hold my phone for a minute, and I gave her Viola's one. Nora did, of course, why wouldn't she and then her prints were all over it. I made sure to hold it by the top and wiped my prints off after."

"That was very good," Mary said appreciatively, and the other women nodded.

"And you nudged us towards Hailey for a while, didn't you?" Bernie prompted.

Tryss shrugged. "I suppose I just wanted the attention on someone else. And Viola and Hailey were arguing on the train. Mind you, Viola argued with everyone, didn't she? She was, well, a bit of a cow."

It was amazing how hesitant Trystesse was to badmouth the woman she had brutally murdered, Bernie thought.

"And you... you hoped that the police would focus on someone else?" Mary suggested.

"It worked, didn't it? They arrested Nora. Although I knew it was too good to be true. I've never been a lucky person."

"It would have been unlucky for the innocent woman who went to jail instead of you," Bernie reminded her.

"I suppose so," Tryss said.

"How did you manage to get Nora's nail polish on the pillow," Liz asked.

Tryss's face brightened. "That was easy. One of her tacky fake nails had fallen off that evening. I had picked it up and put it in my pocket so I could put it in the bin, then I forgot about it. I rubbed it into the pillow, hoping that it would point towards Nora and it did."

Walker came back inside. "The car's here. Will you come with me, Tryss?"

"Good thing that gun wasn't loaded, eh?" Bernie said to the police officer as he led their suspect outside.

"What are you talking about?" Walker replied. "It had live ammunition in it. I've called for the firearms squad to take it away."

304

"Oh," Bernie said, her throat suddenly dry. "So she really could have shot me?"

"Yes. Lucky for us, she didn't," Walker said.

"Aye, or you would have lost your top investigator," Bernie said proudly.

Walker gave her one of his best glares. "That. Or it could be that if a civilian got shot on my watch I would never have lived it down. It would have been even worse than the tank."

Epilogue

Modern policing being what it was, it wasn't until all the paperwork was done on Tuesday night that Walker was allowed to make his way back to Invergryff. It was nearly eleven before he got home. Still, he knew he wanted to see Mary, even if it was just for a few minutes. They had hardly managed any time together in Aviemore, and he was conscious that a good boyfriend should make an effort when their girlfriend's friend had been murdered.

The kids would be in bed, but he hoped that Mary might be still up. He drove up to the house, only to see that all the lights were still on. He got out of the car and walked up to the front door. The living room curtains were shut but he could hear laughing and what sounded like seventies disco music.

He rang the bell. Mary answered the door wearing glitter-ball earrings, a sequined red dress and bunny rabbit slippers. Even for her, it was an outfit that left an impression.

"I thought they would be asleep," Walker said, raising his voice so that Mary could hear him over the music.

"They should be really," she said, giving Lauren a kiss on her forehead when she came up to her and sending her back to the dance. "But they said they missed me and they didn't want to go straight to bed. So I thought it was time for a living room disco."

"Ah," Walker hadn't realised that was a thing.

306

"Let's go into the kitchen. Five more minutes, kids, then bedtime," Mary said, not that any of the children so much as looked around.

"Tea?" Mary asked.

"Better not. I just wanted to pop in to see how you were doing." Walker noticed that her cheeks were pink from jumping around the living room and thought she looked like she was doing pretty great.

"Well, my legs are tired from the dancing," Mary said.

"I meant how you were after the weekend."

"Ah. Well, I don't quite know how to feel. Viola dying was dreadful, of course. And we all sort of went into WWC mode without really thinking about it. I probably shouldn't be having a disco, should I?"

Her eyes dropped to the floor. Walker brushed his hand against her cheek, then kissed her.

"I don't think you should feel guilty about having fun with your kids," Walker said when he pulled away.

"It's like, when something like this happens, you want to hold the ones you love closer to you, do you know what I mean?"

Walker put his arm around her shoulder and felt her warm skin on his.

"I understand."

"Have I mentioned how awesome it was that you came to

rescue us?"

He grinned. "Not enough times. And you lot did pretty well yourselves. Nora is released and the person that killed Viola Gordon has been arrested."

Mary shivered. "Do you know what I can't stand? That Rickey Callford and her cronies are going to get away with all this. I mean, Tryss was the killer, but that lot drove her to it."

Walker shrugged. "The whole case has been passed onto to the fraud department. They may not get away with it for long."

Mary smiled, that smile that warmed his chest. "That is good to hear."

The sounds of Jailhouse Rock floated through from the living room.

"Oh god, that will always remind me of the stripper," Mary said.

"What do you mean?"

"Nothing," she giggled. "Do you know, I don't think I'm ever going to go on another hen-do. They're never that fun, even if there's not a murder."

"Did you have a hen-do? I mean, before you married Matt?"

"Yeah, it was worse than Viola's."

"Worse? How could it be worse?"

"There was a party bus. I'd rather not talk about it."

Walker laughed. "Maybe go for something quieter for your next one?"

"Oh god, never again. And then after the hen-do there is the bigger problem. The marriage. Believe me, been there, done that, still paying off the debt to prove it."

"Right."

Mary gave him a sharp look. "You weren't thinking…"

"No, no. Of course not. Outdated institution, isn't it. Total waste of time." Why was he stumbling over his words? He had never even thought about the idea of marriage. So why did it make his stomach flip over when Mary said she wouldn't consider it?

Mary was about to ask him something else, when a small figure in a tutu appeared in the doorway.

"Is Walker going to sing a song with us?"

"I don't sing," Walker said firmly. Some lines should never be crossed.

"Maybe he could stay the night?" Mary asked, giving Walker a wink.

"Like a sleepover?" Vikki asked. "Can he stay in our room?"

Mary grinned. "Maybe not."

Walker squeezed his girlfriend's arm. "I'd love to stay, if it's okay with your mum."

"All right," Vikki said, grabbing his hand. "But you have to dance the Macarena first."

Mary burst out laughing as he was dragged towards the living room.

"That's always the deal," she called after him. "Macarena, then bedtime."

Afterword

Thank you for reading another wee adventure from the ladies of the Wronged Women's Co-operative.

This novel was inspired by how dreadful most hen-do's are. I always find them terribly awkward: why would school friends, Uni friends, friends from the knitting circle etc. ever get on when all thrust together in a third-rate bar with some very cheap booze? And I got to thinking – what could possibly make a hen-do even more dreadful? What if someone was murdered?

I have never seen a murder committed on a hen-do, but I have seen many people come close! So brides-to-be be warned: choose your friends carefully, and if in doubt, a quiet evening in your local pub might be a better idea than a weekend in a cottage in the middle of nowhere.

The fifth book in this series is available to order now.

Printed in Dunstable, United Kingdom